Double Blank

By the Author

In the Name of God

Wolf Dreams

Morituri

Yasmina Khadra

DOUBLE BLANK

The Toby Press

First English language Edition 2005

The Toby Press LLC, 2004
POB 8531, New Milford, CT. 06676-8531, USA
& POB 2455, London WIA 5WY, England
www.tobypress.com

Originally published as *Double blanc* (Éditions
Baleine, Instantanés de Polar, 1997); republished by
Gallimard (Collection Folio Policier, 2002)

Translation copyright © Aubrey Botsford 2004

Copyright © 2005

ISBN 1 59264 119 9, *paperback original*

A CIP catalogue record for this title is
available from the British Library

Typeset in Garamond by Jerusalem Typesetting

Printed and bound in the United States
by Thomson-Shore Inc., Michigan

*A glossary of some of the Arabic terms used
in this book may be found at the end*

Chapter one

I first knew Ben Ouda in Ghardaïa, just after Independence, which is to say, when homes were abandoned and the judicial system was a void.

In those days I was being initiated into Criminal Investigation's dirty tricks, my head filled with B movies and buzzing with tangled conspiracies. My ambition was to surpass my own heroes. And even though Ghardaïa was just a hamlet with no tales to tell, easy to overlook among the mirages of the desert, I was content to round up street musicians, harass down-and-outs, and generally hunt with the pack to show my superiors how hard I worked.

Ben Ouda was applying to become Sub-prefect. At twenty-eight years of age he was already equipped with both glistening baldness and an impressive girth, which made him credible to a populace for whom a smooth cranium bespoke wisdom and a large gut commanded respect in its own right.

He was a clever man. He knew exactly what he wanted and how to get it. Sometimes, when certain doors were closed to him, he would threaten to obtain a bunch of keys from his relations in Algiers and, as if by magic, doors would suddenly open wide.

But Ben was determined to forge a name for himself, to command admiration from some and surrender from others. So he never missed an opportunity to mention that he was one of the few high school graduates in the country or that books without pictures held no more mysteries for him than the workings of the Administration. He was ambitious, so he registered at Constantine University, and without having to leave his office in the Sahara and thanks to remarkable telepathic powers, he secured a first degree and a doctorate with an ease that remains astonishing.

He was bright, Ben. I remember how a lamb roast would always bring him to the inner circle, where he used to talk so eloquently that his fellow diners would leave the table still hungry. He knew better than anyone how to make connections between poets and conquerors and the brave artisans of our liberation, how to elevate a man's homeland to the heights of Olympus. And listening to him! Shit, you thought yourself part of the Revolution; you felt as if a toss of your head could make the earth tremble!

For an energetic cop like me, raring to go when I came out of the *maquis*, he represented Algeria on the march, martial and triumphant. He was more than my idol—he was my faith. All he had to do was walk past the station and I would be off. I would catch myself pointing him out to my colleagues with the enthusiasm of a schoolboy recognizing his teacher in the *souk*.

So when Ben was brought up on a minor charge of indecent assault, my first thought was that he had been framed. From the bottom of my soul, I categorically refused to believe that a *mujahid* of the Sub-prefect's stamp could possibly fall for a snot-nosed fourteen year old. I fought body and soul to clear his name, threatening witnesses and promising reprisals against the victim's parents that would have put off Tamberlane himself.

Ben Ouda was a gentleman. He never forgot my muscular intervention on his behalf. The proof: after thirty years of silence, he remembered me and asked me to come and see him at 14, place de la Charité.

He had come a long way since he was Sub-prefect in Ghardaïa. He had been a magistrate and then a diplomat. He came back in '89 to give a helping hand to the grandees who had been asked by the Raïs to polish up the constitution, to add legitimacy to the all-consuming fundamentalism that would later devour our guts. Rumor has it that he was offered a government portfolio, but his excessive humility suggested he contented himself with his Swiss safety-deposit boxes.

Ben had the reputation of being an intellectual. He prefers the open spaces to mixing with the herd, the tranquility of an overseas residence to the trumpet blasts of protocol. Modestly, he accepted a consulship in black Africa, then they moved heaven and earth so that he wouldn't turn down an ambassadorship in the Orient.

Nostalgia revived his memory, homesickness turned his gilded exile into a retreat, his solitude into a penance, and so it was that one fine day, his books began to appear in the bookstores.

This was in '92. The country was giving birth to a democracy of sorts; the people were praising breakers of taboos, cheering conjurers of truths. In the general frenzy, everyone was jockeying for status. Ben Bella gave us his *Memoirs,* Aït Amed, *The Mesli Affair,* Belaïd Abdeslem, *Algerian Gas.* There was something for everyone.

Ben Ouda, for his part, published *Dream and Utopia*; for us it was an astonishing indictment of the scientific socialism of the donkey trainers who had become the relics of a decadent nation. A bestseller. A few bad comedians even went so far as to suggest that the High Committee of the State, lacking credibility, intended to co-opt the author as a member. And Ben, while the police were being jeered in the streets, made the following legendary declaration: "I love my people too much to oppress them."

I had stopped believing in fakirs, and I said to Mina, "That guy is one of a kind. He doesn't mince his words, which means he's got something solid between his teeth."

Mina didn't appreciate my metaphor. Obscenities upset her.

ॐ

Number 14, place de la Charité, is a magnificent architectural gem built in the middle of a futuristic square. The common folk, the riff-raff, never venture here for fear they'll be carted off as strays. Magnificent gardens on one side, a parking lot studded with big cars on the other. Envious types in my class would have a heart attack on the spot.

Even the concierge is dressed to the nines. Obsequious and then some. Accustomed to fat tips, he's quite capable of disturbing a dying man on a drip feed at three o'clock in the morning just to cheer him up with a smile.

"May I be of service, sir?" he says, with that hypocritical gallantry that educated people call courtesy.

"If you've nothing better to do, my car gets scared when it's left all by itself. Maybe you could hold its hand until I get back."

He accepts willingly, the poor bastard.

At fifty-eight, Ben Ouda has tripled in volume. The facelifts have not succeeded in hiding the wrinkles in his face, and his belly pours anarchically over his knees. I think he must have to use shock-absorbers to assist his braces.

He receives me in his living room, which is that of a privileged man of independent means. Without ceremony, as you might receive an old friend.

"A glass of orange juice, Mister Llob?"

"I'm on duty."

He offers me an armchair and spreads out on a couch opposite me. His robe glitters. Faced with his obesity, I am momentarily lost in a dream, wondering whether, if we're honest, nature isn't just having a laugh at some people's expense.

"I hope I'm not taking up too much of your time, Superintendent. We all know how busy you are—this war shows no signs of abating."

"It's not a problem."

He frowns and puts his head to one side to examine me from another angle.

"Haven't we met before somewhere?"

His lapse of memory astonishes me. But this kind of amnesia is common currency with us. It seems to grease the wheels.

"I don't think so," I retort, piqued.

"But your manner…"

"I look like anyone else from the Kabyl tribe. I'm often taken for someone else."

He doesn't pursue it.

He is holding a glass of whiskey delicately in his fleshy hand and brings it to his lips.

"My friends tell me good things about you, Mister Llob. Most of all, they say you're a man you can count on."

"No better than credit."

He laughs. Just a spasm. Like the gods. He puts down his glass and looks me right in the eye.

"Your last book caught my attention. I read it twice."

"You're too kind."

"I agree entirely with your analysis, Mister Llob."

I'm looking at a painting by Dinet on the wall between two damascene swords and wondering what the hell a work listed as part of our national heritage is doing in a private apartment.

Ben Ouda swallows another mouthful and smacks his lips. His belly protrudes from his robe when he straightens his legs.

"Do you believe in destiny, Mister Llob?"

"It has its points."

He shakes his head pensively.

"I sometimes think I'm predestined to do something, don't you?"

I smother a yawn with my hand.

He goes on: "For years I've had this bee in my bonnet, only I haven't had the motivation. It's usually hard to get me to do anything. But the situation in this country is getting more and more complicated; that's why recently I've been tormented by the desire to react. Alas! Every time I feel ready to do something, my ideas seem inconsequential, inopportune, suicidal. Fortunately, your book fell into my hands. When I finished it, I knew I wasn't alone and I decided to make a stand, once and for all. There's something that's rotten in our state has no name. We simply have to mobilize ourselves to expose the causes and effects of this absurd tragedy."

He is interrupted by the opening of a door. I turn and discover a young man of uncommon beauty, feminine of face, with large, sky-blue eyes.

"Oh, I'm sorry!" he apologizes.

Ben is annoyed at this intrusion. His jowls flush red. The kid hurries out of the room, closing the door carefully behind him.

I pretend not to have noticed anything compromising and cross my legs again to appear relaxed.

Ben stands up and goes out onto the balcony. The breeze ruffles the few whitening hairs at his temples. He leans hazardously on the balustrade and looks out over the bay, which is lined with blank white buildings.

"Come over here, Mister Llob."

I make the best of it and join him.

He points to Algiers with a theatrical gesture. "Look at this city. It's crumbling into insignificance: impersonal, anonymous, commonplace. It looks like an architect's model with woodworm. And yet its sky has no equal anywhere else. Its sun is orgasmic, its night idyllic. This country is thirsty for drunkenness. It's made for celebration."

Together we look at the haze-tinged port, Notre-Dame d'Afrique champing at the bit at the top of its hill, the casbah like a moth-eaten shroud, and I have no idea what he's getting at.

"And look at the result of thirty unhappy years of insanity. Dangerous streets, Dumpsters everywhere you look, and a mentality fit to make the finest MRI scanner blow a fuse. Terrible, don't you think?"

He is becoming sadder and turns to me as his witness.

His voice quavers: "Once upon a time, history used our monuments as her copybook and centaurs quenched their thirst in our mothers' fields. Prophets bowed down before our long-suffering patience in the face of adversity. Only yesterday, mythology was weaving its cloth from the tresses of our widows, and the beauty of the horizon was born of our orphans' gaze. And now look what we're reduced to: We're nobody. Ignoble wanderers. That's all we are."

His voice rises three octaves as he bangs his fist on the railing. "So now a race of giants is being replaced by a pretty strange colony of hermit crabs, their shells filled with bile and putrefaction."

He grips my shoulders as we used to do in the *maquis.*

"I'd like to put this all down on paper, Mister Llob. That's why I asked to see you."

I extract myself from his grip as best I can and go back into the living room.

"You don't have to decide right away, Mister Llob."

"I must admit, I'm taken by surprise. Why me?"

"Why not you?"

That's not good enough for me.

After thirty years of hand-to-hand combat with disappointment, I'm certain that nothing in our country happens by coincidence.

I'm reminded of a recent shouting match with my boss. Were they trying to test my recidivist tendencies? Ever since it became obvious that terrorism was a real force in our society, nobody's mad enough to trust anyone else. It's every man for himself. In the general panic, no one knows who's who.

"I have in my possession an irrefutable document," he says, trying to hook me. "Codename N.S.O. A plan the devil himself couldn't have foreseen."

He grabs my wrist and promptly lets it go again.

He shakes his head.

"These are great unknowns, Llob my friend. You're more likely to survive in a nest of vipers than in our country. But it doesn't matter whether we keep quiet or shout from the rooftops: it's not *our* attitude that motivates *them.*"

"I know."

"So there's no point in keeping quiet."

He looks right at me. His sincerity frightens me. The distress of our masters is an apocalypse.

"Our country needs neither prophets nor a president. It needs an exorcist. Think about it, Mister Llob, take your time."

Abruptly, I offer him my hand. "Goodbye, Mister Ouda."

He hesitates before offering his.

"Glad to have made your acquaintance, Superintendent."

He accompanies me out to the landing and calls the elevator.

"The chaotic state of affairs in our country is a sign of troubled waters—the monsters of the deep can do what they like. This appalling scenario has gone on long enough. I need to know what you decide as soon as possible."

"You'll have it soon, I promise you."

The elevator arrives.

Ben prevents the doors from taking me away. His eyes hold mine for a long time.

"We must *change* all this, Mister Llob. It must *change*."

A shudder starts in his chest and climbs through the three chins leading up to his jaw, while a great sadness takes hold behind his smile.

The doors of the elevator close.

ₐₑ

A long time ago I worshipped a man. He was a good man. He was as good as white bread, and when he took me on his knee, I was in heaven. I've forgotten the color of his eyes, the smell of his body; I've even forgotten his face, but I shall remember every word he said. He could say things as if fate had dictated them. He could make me believe in the things he believed in. Maybe he was a saint. He was convinced that with a little humility men could survive leviathans and great oceans. It upset him to see men looking elsewhere for things that were within their reach. It was because he so wanted to *change* the world that he died, because he alone had not changed.

Chapter two

Agiant built like a brick wall crosses the threshold of the police station. His shoulders brush against both sides of the corridor, forcing staff members to flatten themselves against the walls. He is so tall that the orderly has to crick his neck to scrutinize him. Skull completely shaven, forehead square, eyebrows level with eyelashes—the air swirls around him.

As the colossus proceeds, typewriters stop clacking one after another, and heads appear in doorways to check that the Terminator who just went by wasn't a hallucination.

Bahia, the secretary, is organizing files when the light is blotted out around her. She almost falls off the stepladder when she notices the Goliath stuck in the doorframe. Her hands remain in the air for a moment, then she squeaks out, "Yes?"

"I'm looking for Superintendent Llob."

Bahia is startled by the sound of the giant's voice, which is as abrupt and powerful as a charging bull; the voice of maleness, virility incarnate.

"Who shall I say is calling?"

"Ewegh Seddig."

"Ah, you must be the para."

She straightens her clothing.

"It's on your left."

Ewegh turns on the spot, like a tank. Bahia has just enough time to measure the breadth of his shoulders, to weigh up the strength of his arms.

"Now that's what I call a man!" she is heard to simper.

I stand up to greet the giant.

Lino pretends to file his nails.

"You're on time. That's already a point in your favor. Please sit down."

Ewegh can't decide between the regular chair and the armchair. Lino, who has a problem with behemoths, looks up at him blandly and says, sarcastically, "Make sure there's no detonator pin on the seat, unless you want us picking you up in pieces with a teaspoon."

Ewegh pays no attention to the lieutenant's sarcasm. The chair protests under his carcass.

Lino drops his nail clippers, crosses his legs, and pretends to be interested in the portrait of the Raïs above my head.

He starts in again. "Who cut your hair? The gardener?"

Ewegh keeps his chin up. Hands braced against his thighs, he hasn't appeared to notice the presence of the lieutenant even once.

Ever since the death of Inspector Serdj,* Lino has been unpleasant to everyone. His bitterness has even driven him to grow a ponytail, which makes it look as though he's trying to piss the Republic off. In reality, he's trying to put the fundamentalists off the scent.

His unorthodox look hasn't endeared him to his superiors. But Lino has developed a trick: at the slightest criticism, he plays the depression card. What's more, he boasts, he has filled his shoes with sticks of dynamite in case some incautious fanatic should take it into his head to tread on his toes.

I leaf through the giant's file: thirty-seven years old. Single.

---

* In *Morituri*, the volume in Yasmina Khadra's Inspector Llob series that preceded this one, Inspector Serdj is gruesomely decapitated.

Highly qualified instructor at the National Police Academy. Two commendations. Three diplomas. One reprimand and a hefty wad of warnings.

"Ewegh, that's an uncommon name."

"I'm a Tuareg."

"What made you put in for a transfer—the Academy canteen? You don't often see people giving up the peace of a training center for the hassle of an operational unit."

He cracks his knuckles one by one, the rest of his body tense as a board.

He says evenly, "Thirty-five percent of the cops I trained got beaten up as soon as they went on duty. I concluded that my methods were out of date and decided to go back into the field."

This makes Lino snicker in a superior manner, then say, "I hear you were in the paras for seven years. Why were you discharged? Because you fell out of a tree?"

"Because I discharged a guy who thought his rank gave him supernatural powers."

"Yes, I understand you're a bit of a hothead."

The Tuareg's gaze shifts to the lieutenant, then returns to where it was.

"Sometimes."

Bahia interrupts us on the pretext that there's a word she can't read in a report I gave her to type. While I explain it to her, she keeps looking over at the colossus. Lino feels his veins start to bulge with jealousy.

"What's the matter, honey? Can't read your boss's handwriting?"

Bahia doesn't push it. She gathers up the draft and makes herself scarce.

I close the file, take my jacket off its hook, and get up.

"Welcome to Club Llob, Ewegh Seddig. You're just in time for dinner. Might as well throw you in at the deep end."

༺

The tour of the eateries takes us to Bab el-Oued. On the way, I describe the sector to the new recruit, paying particular attention to the hot spots, the hostile bistros, and the underground brothels where the higher-ups of sedition come for relaxation.

Ewegh, spread out on the backseat, just grumbles. From time to time he fidgets, and from this I conclude that his radar has detected a beard.

"Are they all in our files, these pube-faces in their robes?" he asks at length.

"Down to their chinny-chin-chins," says Lino gleefully, one foot unashamedly pressed to the windshield.

The giant zips his lips tight to his gums. Only his knuckles continue to crack.

Sid Ali's ptomaine palace infests the corner of rue du Pont, facing a devastated square swarming with noisy kids. It's a cave, fifteen feet by twenty-five, with a homemade counter on one side displaying a variety of dubious-looking kebabs and on the other side, some tables surrounded by crippled chairs. At the back of the room, a portrait of Cheb Hasni smiles at a poster of Belloumi. On the rough-and-ready shelves hanging over the cash register, among the trophies and pennants, there are photographs spotted with fly shit, showing the owner of this dive posing with the Mouloudia soccer team or glowing with pride next to some former hero of the ring.

As soon as our unmarked car pulls up alongside the curb, Sid Ali wolfs down his sandwich so as not to have to share it, wipes his hands on his apron, and steps out to welcome us.

He leaps on me with the enthusiasm of a former cop turned snack vendor.

"How's it going, you old joker?" he cries, slobbering on my cheeks.

"It's going."

He steps back to admire my gut and buries an affectionate fist in it.

"When's it due?"

"The doctor says it's a hysterical pregnancy."

The owner throws his head back and neighs and then, struck by Ewegh's bulk, inquires, "Where did you dig him up, a cave?"

"He was in a bottle."

"You don't say! What do you feed him?"

At this point he turns his attention to Lino, who's pretending to check his heels so as to show off his hairdo.

"Who's this Taras Bulba arriving from the Sahel?"

"It's Lino, for goodness' sake!"

"You're kidding! Has he ever changed! He's hidden a barrel of gunpowder behind his face, though, am I right?"

"What makes you come up with such a dumb idea?" says Lino through gritted teeth. He hates being belittled in front of a rival.

"Well, that slow fuse hanging off the back of your head."

"It's a ponytail. And that's just the tip of the iceberg. You should see the one that's hidden."

I lean against the counter and move on to business.

"So, how's the neighborhood?"

"De-con-taminated, Superintendent. It's been ages since we glimpsed the shadow of even a trace of a true believer in this sector. We've got our act together since the booby-trapped truck. If so much as a cockroach turns up in the gutter, it's numbered and catalogued on the spot."

"Delighted to hear it."

"What about the guy who used to rant out curses in '66?" Lino interjects, to steal a march on the rookie.

Sid Ali goes behind the counter and chases some flies off the skewers of meat with a swatter. Then he says, "He's kept a low profile ever since we shaved his beard off at the station. He says hello when he comes by, and nobody gives him the time of day. We've had enough of gurus around here."

I examine a bottle of lemonade, decide it's a rather strange color, and put it down.

"I hear some strange birds make their nests at the Sharif *hammam*."

Sid Ali waves reassuring commas in the air with his hand. "Guys from the high plateau. They work at the biscuit factory on the corner. We've reported them. They're clean."

The dispatcher calls us.

Lino runs over, then signals to me to join him.

"Trouble, Super."

"Hey!" says Sid Ali. "I haven't had a customer all morning. At least take something to eat."

"Sore throat, my friend. Bye. And keep your eyes open. Keep in touch."

⁊

Three police cars are pointlessly flashing their blue lights outside number 14, place de la Charité. Inspector Bliss is there, sitting on the hood of a car, an imported cigarette perched on his lower lip.

Protected as he is by the big boss, he doesn't even bother to alter his posture. His hypocritical eyes show me the way:

"The team's already up there," he tells me between puffs, signifying that the whole thing is a matter of indifference to him.

I cherish two dreams for the twilight of my career: to enjoy my retirement in the possession of all my faculties and to shove this piece of shit into a microwave until his skull disintegrates.

I can think of no worse disease than to be treated with disdain by a well-connected subordinate.

The fifth-floor landing is flooded with tentacle-like pools of blood. In some places it has reached the stairs. Lino has to walk with his back against the wall so as not to dirty his espadrilles.

Cops are busy all over the place, looking for clues, while a photographer covers the whole area with frantic machine-gun-like flashes. Ben Ouda is in the hallway, his arms crossed, his head cut off. A grotesque axe, stained with brownish goop, lies on the sofa.

"His head's in the bidet, in the bathroom," a sergeant tells me as he wipes his vomit-stained tunic with a cloth. "If this continues, in a few generations people will be born with nothing between their shoulders."

"What makes you think they've got anything there now?"

Lino isn't feeling well. He sees butchery like this every day, but he can't get used to it. He leans on a table and lights a cigarette to stop himself from throwing up.

14

The sergeant adds, "There's a guy in the wardrobe. He won't come out."

I follow him into the bedroom, which is painted pink and has nudes on the walls and flowers in the alcoves. The wardrobe is on the left, its doors folded back. I crouch down. The guy is cringing in the back of the wardrobe, his head between his thighs, trembling so hard his teeth are chattering.

"Come on out, son. It's all over."

It's Ben Ouda's boy toy. He's in a terrible state: pale, petrified, and not seeming to understand what I say. I hold out my hand. He makes a gurgling sound and retreats somewhat further into his bit of shadow.

"Let's go, come out. The bogeyman's gone."

His muscles tense beneath my fingers. I draw him toward me cautiously. He allows himself to be led like a child. The sergeant helps him to sit on the bed and offers him a glass of water. The boy doesn't have the strength to lift his arm. He stares at us dementedly.

Suddenly he starts raving. "I never thought a man could scream like that. It's impossible to scream like he screamed. I don't think I'll ever get his screaming out of my head!"

I ask the sergeant to take care of the poor bastard and go back into the living room. Lino has collapsed on the sofa, his hair in disarray. He's staring at the ceiling and hasn't noticed that his cigarette has gone out.

In the bathroom, the photographer is immortalizing the *thing* in the bottom of the bidet. I move closer. The diplomat's head is the stuff of nightmares.

"Be careful, Superintendent," the photographer warns me, "it's booby-trapped. The bomb's just underneath it."

He points out a wire that has been carefully concealed under the seat.

"Has anyone contacted the bomb squad?"

"They'll be here any minute."

Ben Ouda's office looks as though a tornado's hit it. The bookshelf is on the floor, there are tipped-out drawers among the mass of papers. The door of a small wall safe hangs open: the inside has been rifled through.

"There are neighbors opposite, neighbors below, and neighbors above, but despite all the racket, nobody heard a thing."

"Yeah, right," an officer sighs. "*Après moi le déluge.*"

The boy doesn't even begin to recover his spirits until after the bomb squad has left. In the meantime, the ambulance crew has taken the remains away.

I bring over a chair and sit opposite the boy.

"Are you okay?"

He assents weakly with his chin.

"What's your name?"

"Salem Toufik."

"How old are you?"

"Nineteen."

"Do you recognize me?"

"Yes."

"What happened?"

His eyes go blank.

I take his hand quickly.

"If you're not up to talking, don't worry. We can continue later."

"I want to get the hell out of here," he sobs. "It's a madhouse. You don't kill people like that. I want to get out of this town, right now."

"How many were there?"

"Three or four. I don't remember."

"Did you know them?"

"We don't entertain bums here."

"They were bums?"

"They were...they were..." He puts his head between his hands. "I want to wake up, I want to wake up, I want to wake up..."

I give him fifteen seconds to steady himself and then continue. "The quicker you fill us in, the more chance we have of catching them."

He flicks his hair back and breathes in. He crumples the bed-
clothes with his hands.

"The doorbell rang. Ben went to see who it was. I was in the
bedroom and I saw them bundle him in with their weapons. I ran
and hid in the wardrobe. One guy came in to check the bedroom. He
didn't see me. He went back into the living room. Ben was getting
angry. He ordered them to get out of the house, threatened to call
the police. I think they hit him. I heard him fall to the ground. They
were yelling, 'Where's the diskette?' Ben said he didn't know what they
were talking about. They threw themselves on him. He was screaming
like it was the end of the world. He screamed so much I passed out…
Tell me none of this is true. Wake me up, I beg you."

The rest of his lament was a series of long moans.

"He's all yours," I tell the sergeant.

With a nod I tell Lino and Ewegh to follow me.

Outside, night is descending on the city like an embittered
and frigid enchantress reclining in a bed of nettles. In a sky riddled
with elusive reference points, the moon is going all out to be a bad
omen, and in the far distance, among the gauzy shadows of the sea,
a rejected ocean liner has transformed itself into a firefly; not that
anyone's taken in by its party trick. It is the time at which people
hide themselves away to craft excuses, their consciences padlocked
shut, an opaque slumber over their eyes. Algiers has again turned into
hell; her patron saints no longer help her. Her nightfalls are funereal.
The slightest rustling is felt as a cry of agony.

Chapter three

The building housing the security service's Communications Center plays its cards close to its chest. No rubberneck would ever guess that one of the most effective information centers on the continent operates from behind the ruins of this disused factory.

I came here once before, during Superintendent Din's time as head of the computer department. I still shiver when I think about it. A guard disguised in rags lets me through the gate and guides me through a maze of miscellaneous junk. There's a trapdoor, and then there's another guard, this time in a suit and tie, who confiscates my papers, enters me in a register, and hustles me into the pitch darkness.

There's no time to leave a trail of white pebbles—an elevator swallows me up, then spits me out like tainted food into a corridor worthy of an operating theatre. No need for an escort here. Rotating cameras X-ray you, and your instincts lead you by the nose toward your destiny.

My guard looks like a benevolent tribal chieftain. He wears his Cobra sunglasses with the same dignity with which he carries his fifty years. He has the build of a milestone and a smile that would seem inoffensive in a sanatorium, and yet his person radiates such authority and suspicion that you come to doubt your own shadow.

He comes out of his austere office, shakes my hand, notices my unease, and tries to reassure me. "Just a few formalities. Do sit down. Superintendent."

The telephone chimes in. My host begs me to excuse him. He listens for a long time in silence, hangs up, and comes back to me, leaving his smile behind with the receiver.

I kill off a packet of cigarettes. He advises me to give up. To feel me out, doubtless.

"Your boss has of course told you that we're interested in the Ben Ouda affair. The deceased was an extremely influential diplomat. We have reason to believe that his elimination is a sign that there is a great deal at stake politically. You've read the newspapers this morning. Speculation is rife, and that annoys the powers that be. I don't know whether you know the latest: the only witness we have, Salem Toufik, the boy he lived with, threw himself off the fifth floor yesterday evening."

"I know."

He spreads a copy of the late Salem Toufik's statement out on the table and taps a key word with his finger.

"What did he mean by 'diskette,' Superintendent?"

"No idea."

"You didn't try to find out more?"

"The kid was in a state of shock."

"You should have persisted."

"The idea was to pick up our little chat later."

"That was unfortunate. Seeing as he killed himself."

"That's bad luck."

My imperturbability is annoying him.

He puts the copy back in a folder, sticks his nose in my face and goes on the attack:

"What were you doing at Ben Ouda's place two days before his murder?"

I am struck dumb for five seconds.

"He asked me to come and see him."

"Why?"

"To talk."

"About what?"

"Birds."

He drums his fingers on his shirt. His jaws clench, then immediately relax.

Calmly, he says, "You're a cop. You know what this means."

"That I'm the prime suspect?"

"Cooperation at last. Did you know each other?"

"We saw a bit of each other in Ghardaïa in '65."

"Were you in the habit of meeting?"

"No."

"Why this time?"

"He had just read my book. He wanted to congratulate me."

He strokes his moustache.

He's not convinced.

"He didn't seem worried to you?"

"Don't think so."

"He didn't mention the 'diskette'?"

"No."

"What about documents, or anything else along those lines?"

"Look, I left my omelette on the stove and I haven't had breakfast yet. My visit to Ben Ouda was just a courtesy call. He was killed on my turf. I promise I'll inform you of the outcome of my investigation. Right now, your air-conditioning is beginning to disorient me. My home is next to some empty lot, if you follow me."

To my great surprise, he rings for the guard and asks him to take me back.

We parted without another word, without a handshake. Before I left, I turned around. What I saw in his eyes started me thinking.

❧

I spent the next week nearly destroying my cervical vertebrae from looking behind me. I had the constant feeling I was being tailed. And although I was expecting the sky to fall on my head, it was actually a second stiff that fell into my arms.

A crowd has gathered on rue Ferhan Saïd and is silently watching the cops busying themselves around the villa at number 18.

Bliss is crouched in front of a bullet-riddled car, staring at the keys on the ground.

"They didn't even give him time to open the door."

"Who was he?" I ask, exasperated by the dwarf's talent for being everywhere at once.

"Abad, Nasser, sixty-seven, bachelor. He was a professor at Benak University."

"Exit one more intellectual," sighs Lino.

"According to the witnesses, there were three of them," Bliss goes on. "One of them stayed in the car. The other two chased the victim into the courtyard of the villa. There are some shells there, and indoors. Probably from a Kalashnikov. It happened at about one o'clock. The professor was about to go back to Benak."

The body of the professor is crumpled on the doorstep, his glasses smashed on the road. He's an old man, white-haired, tall and thin, with chiseled features. He's lifting the collar of his coat with his left hand, as if this absurd defensive reflex could have protected him against the volley of bullets

"They were in a gray Peugeot," Bliss continues, to show us he has left no stone unturned. "I've passed the registration number to Dispatch."

"Thanks. Dismissed."

The brusqueness of my tone makes him gulp. He disappears. It's like a break in the clouds. Freed of his malign influence, I have space to concentrate on the drama.

Before he gave up the ghost, the victim wrote something on the step. The blood has thickened, but the path of his finger can be traced: "HIV," I read.

"Do you have any birdies left in the box?" I turn to the photographer.

"A whole nestful, boss."

"Do me a close-up of these strange initials."

"Don't touch anything!" a voice rages in falsetto.

A runt squeezed into a tight suit like a two-bit mafioso shoves aside the cop on duty at the door to the villa and rushes toward me, his badge held up like a crucifix in front of a vampire.

"Captain Berrah, Communications. My team will be here any minute. Get your traveling circus out of here and leave, pronto."

"Take it easy, Captain. You're frightening us."

"I don't give a damn. Pack your bags, Superintendent, and clear off."

Lino's had enough. "One more word from you, you little pipsqueak, and you'll be the one packing his bags."

He's stunned, our cousin in the service. He frowns, completely thrown by this insolence from a subordinate, looks at me, and, indicating Lino with his thumb, asks, "Where did this kid spring from?"

"Jupiter's ass," I tell him.

Playing the role of the offended gods, the captain stares up to heaven, then down at the ground, and then asks me again, leaving his thumb on his shoulder. "What was it he called me?"

"Pipsqueak," Lino repeats contemptuously. "Small ass, big mouth."

Only now does the captain consent to face the blasphemer and place his thumb on his chest.

"So I'm a pipsqueak, am I?"

"Yup, you're a pipsqueak."

I try to calm them down, in accordance with Ministry of the Interior circular 129. The captain refuses to let it ride. He's swaying, his face contorted. Without removing his thumb from his chest, he points his index finger at Lino. "You'll be hearing from Berrah soon, young man. And as for that Chink ponytail of yours, I'm going to shave it off with a lawnmower."

"You can shave some other parts while you're about it."

Berrah abruptly reaches under his jacket. An unfortunate and regrettable move: Ewegh's arm instantly extends itself. James Bond 007 executes a double somersault and ends up flat out on the road with a stricken nose.

Groggily, he mumbles, "I was only getting out my pen to write down his badge number."

To which Ewegh replies imperturbably, "I thought he was pulling a piece."

Which, to him, is sufficient justification for what he's done.

⁂

The sun has been making life complicated for itself behind the Maqam column. It would like to be flirting with the clouds but fears it wouldn't be taken seriously. The sky transmits its blue funk downward to the quivering bay. Algiers hoards her suffering the way a wino hoards his rotgut wine. She is huddled up, worn out by the effort of holding back her spasms so that she doesn't explode.

In my stressful office, I'm trying distractedly to drown myself in a cup of coffee. Lino and Ewegh have gone before the disciplinary board to have their knuckles rapped. The first has been charged with insubordination, the second with having seriously damaged the most important tool of the captain's trade, his snout.

I'm worried sick about them, as I unconsciously copy interminable H-I-Vs onto any piece of paper within reach of my gloom.

Bahia has been to see me twice to have a memo explained to her. I didn't understand a word she said.

I'm not well.

Just as matters are coming to a head, the boss enters my lair. With a click of his fingers he commands the secretary to vanish, then confides, "I was with the board ten minutes ago. The chairman's a friend. He's promised to be indulgent."

"It would be a bit irritating if they were publicly castrated," I say with an air of cynicism.

"A minor reprimand, with a bit of luck."

He drops into the armchair, studies the intertwining cracks in the ceiling and comes back to the subject of my disgust. "The situation is serious, Brahim. We have the most appalling kind of fundamentalism on our hands. It's not in our interest to get into squabbles between forces. Criminal Investigation, Vice, Comms, the enemy doesn't draw distinctions."

24

I light a cigarette and blow the smoke out through my nostrils. The boss moves away slightly to dodge my exhalations.

"Try to frown at your men, Superintendent. I want you to shout at them excessively when they get back. We're in enough shit as it is, and I won't have rotten apples in my department."

He stands up and pretends to remember a detail suddenly.

"I almost forgot. What does your Lino hope to gain by making an exhibition of himself? What's with the hair down his neck? Try to reason with him, for God's sake. All he needs now is tits."

I nod.

"And that giant of yours, are you sure he's all there?" he adds.

"He's got all his faculties, I can vouch for that."

"Tell him to keep some of them under control, please, particularly his fists. He's still new around here."

"I'll see what I can do."

He follows the spiraling smoke and shakes his head imperceptibly. "I saw Captain Berrah this morning. I didn't recognize him. He looks like the door of the Treasury blew shut in his face. Poor man. He'll never be able to wear his Ray Bans again."

"How sad. They do like to keep up appearances at Comms."

He smiles.

It's unusual, but for once it suits him.

Chapter four

Lino has spent the morning in the operations room, alone with his notebook, his ponytail, and his bundles of files, setting the stage and reestablishing his credentials. Around noon, he agrees to receive us. He's put up two boards facing each other. On the left, he's pinned up large-format photos of Ben Ouda and Professor Abad; on the right, those four hirsute individuals who look as though they had long ago consigned razor blades to the category of mortal sin.

Lino waits patiently for me to strip off my jacket, then for the Tuareg and me to sit down on metal chairs, and clears his throat to request silence. A fly starts buzzing. We hold our breath.

He prepares his performance with the concentration of a knife-thrower, as if his career depended on it, abruptly extending his telescopic pen and pointing it at the right-hand board:

"The concierge at 14, place de la Charité, and several eye-witnesses have identified four of the five murderers of the diplomat and the academic. They are: one—Merouan, Sid Ahmed, a.k.a. TNT. A real blot on the landscape. Unmarried. No profession. Originally from Aïn Defla. Involved in both attacks. Two—Blidi, Kamel, thirty years old. Married, four children, junk dealer in El-Harrach. Involved in both attacks. Three—Zaddam, Brahim, thirty-two years old, Afghan veteran. Not involved in the second attack. Four—Gaïd, Ali, a.k.a. the Hairdresser, twenty-five years old, emir of the group. Would empty hell out quicker than the bogeyman would clear a nursery school. Behind the recent series of car-bomb attacks in the capital. Seventeen attacks in eight months."

"Was he a hairdresser by trade?" I inquire, to break his flow.

"He's called that because he cuts off his victims' heads."

Ewegh looks intently at the photo of the "emir."

"Did they know each other, the dip and the prof?"

"Apparently not. They were diametrically opposite types: the diplomat moved among the upper echelons, the academic preferred slumming it."

"Tell us a bit about the prof."

"Not much to say. He was an extremely private guy. No friends. His students called him 'the Tapeworm.' An existence like an equilateral triangle: workplace, bistro, bed. Formerly adviser to Saïd Rufik. Resigned after three months."

"Who's Rafik?"

"The minister of culture, who else?"

"And I thought the only minister of culture who knew Algeria was Jack Lang… What was his reason for resigning?"

"Personality differences."

Bliss pushes open the door of the room and shows his rat-like face, all aglow. "They've found the Peugeot. Lieutenant Chater's on the scene."

I stare at him venomously and say, "So what?"

❧

There are cities that seem to date from the dawn of time but their glory is no more. Their stories have petered out. They're just there to haunt your spirits. Sometimes mothballed museums, sometimes muzzled muses, the sun broods over them, and when day breaks, it breaks on a sleepless night.

The casbah doesn't go back that far in time, but it borrows the same dramas, the same ghosts. Fools can boast about its ruins all they like—but they're just so much rubble.

Suspended between memory and utopia, the casbah silently gnaws away at its torment, complaining that the tide still hasn't swept it away.

Here in this tangled web, resignation rises ceaseless and unconfined, like a noxious dough. People don't expect anything anymore. With their feet in purgatory and their heads in limbo, their prayers are transformed into curses. The graffiti on the walls has the feel of epitaphs. Cobblestones raise bruises on the surface of the disgraced road. Doorways inject their shadows deep into men's minds.

A dumping ground for all misfortunes, the casbah remains besieged by its epic history, like a widow besieged by the love of her martyred husband whose children torment her memory on every street corner.

The Circle of Friends is to the casbah what the exercise yard is to a prison. To reach it, you have to know where to put your feet. It's a squalid, dubious dive. The unemployed come here and sip their coffees, the better to brood, as they wait for the evening so they can die a little. They're there from morning till night, ruining the tables with slapped-down dominoes, turning their backs on the procession of days, on the promises of a homeland without parole. Their faces are dreary, their souls signed over to the realm of renunciation.

They are not pleased to see us turn up. The Tuareg and I install ourselves at the bar. Suddenly, Ewegh's neighbor—a monumental specimen—stops contemplating his brew and starts flapping at the air around him with disgust.

"Which asshole forgot to flush the toilet again?"

Then, noticing the Tuareg on his right, he frowns. "Look! A dinosaur!"

A few sarcastic laughs break out, and the comedian goes on, addressing the barman. "You never told me there was a Chinese circus in town."

"You never asked."

The joker turns back to face Ewegh and eyes him up and down.

With a point of his finger, he pushes him back. "You're in the wrong tent, dino. Piss off, and make it snappy. Hey, dino!"

"You've picked the wrong guy," growls the Tuareg.

"The wrong guy, maybe, but I never get an animal wrong."

The room shakes with exaggerated laughter. Pleased, the comedian pushes Ewegh again. He doesn't have time to think of another joke. Ewegh's arm shoots out, flattening the clown's nose in a single lightning thrust.

An uncomfortable silence falls over the onlookers.

Ewegh grabs the fellow by the scruff of his neck and shows his smashed face to the barman. "Your Chinese circus seems to have misplaced this clown."

The entire clientele swiftly leaves, gathering up what's left of the comedian on the way.

The barman ignores us from behind his counter, an obscene leer at the center of his beard. He's a rather stunted creature, with the face of a cathedral gargoyle, shoulders above his head, and protuberant eyes. There are so many hairs on his face it's as if he's wearing a balaclava. In short, the kind of freak you should never show to elderly people, pregnant women, or well-brought-up children without warning them first.

"Ben Hamid?" I ask him.

"Might be."

For a moment his eyes dart across me.

"A gray Peugeot, registration number 44999.195.16. Is it yours?"

"Might be."

"Was it stolen?"

"I reported it."

"Twenty-four hours later?"

He stops pulling at his beard, grabs a rag, and mechanically polishes the area around him.

He mumbles, "It happened on a Friday."

"The police work every day."

"Friday's my day for prayer. Anything else?"

"We haven't even started."

He tosses the rag on the floor and starts rinsing cups in a sink filled with dirty water.

"You've no right to drive my customers away. This is my bread and butter, this place."

"We didn't drive anyone away. This is a democracy. Kindly tell us what you know about this theft."

"How many police are there in this godforsaken country? I'm not spending my life with one cop after another. I've got better things to do."

My expression hardens.

He puffs out his cheeks in a sign of boredom and wipes the cups with a greasy cloth.

"It was four o'clock in the morning. They broke down the door, put some kind of blunderbuss to my head, and forced me to hand over the ignition keys."

"How many were there?"

"I didn't count."

"Would you recognize them again?"

"It was dark."

"There's a light just in front of your terrace. It's still working. I checked."

"In that case they were wearing masks."

Ewegh stirs. Dangerously. I ask him to hold it in patiently.

The barman snickers, "Does your stuffed gorilla have a problem? He must be pining for his attic."

Ewegh keeps his cool. The barman gives him the eye for a moment, then plunges the cups he's just wiped back into the dirty water.

"You're not welcome here, flatfoot. I'm so allergic to pigs that even the sight of bacon makes me throw up. If that's all, get lost. Some guys relieved me of my wheels. I reported the theft. As far as I'm concerned, that's the end of the story."

"That's the third time it's happened to you in two months."

"So I live in a shitty area. What would you have done with a sawn-off shotgun in your ear?"

I spread out the photos of the four butchers on the bar.

"Could one or two of your attackers be among these?"

He gives the photos a superficial glance and shakes his head. "I don't know who they are."

"Look carefully."

"I'm not nearsighted."

"This one here, the third on the left?"

"Don't know him."

"His name is Gaïd, Ali, alias the Hairdresser. Your neighbor."

"Could be. Anything else?"

"Your car's been recovered."

He doesn't exactly jump with delight, even though the carcass is worth eighty big ones.

"Your neighbor's prints are on it."

"What d'you expect? You can't trust anyone these days."

"Your car was used by Professor Nasser Abad's murderers."

Might as well whisper sweet nothings in a mullah's ear.

He limits himself to examining a glass.

"I reported the theft. It's up to you to take the necessary steps. Anything else?"

"Not for the moment."

Ewegh leans over the counter again.

"My name is Ewegh Seddig and I've got no connection with the Good Samaritan. Tell your badly shaved pals that it's their funeral, and I won't be sending any gifts."

The barman nods contemptuously. "That's right, dino."

I don't have time to prevent the inevitable blow. The Tuareg's fist flashes out. The barman is propelled against the wall, a jigsaw puzzle where his face should be.

"Ewegh, do try to remember: you should only correct people when they call you 'cop,' not 'dino.'"

Chapter five

Take a mummy and change its diaper and you'll end up with the man I found at the Sidi Mabrouk Clinic, room 33.

He's fallen on hard times, Athman Mamar. Not long ago, the slightest twinge would have mobilized half the city around him. Now they hardly bother to take his temperature.

Stretched out on an evil-smelling cot, plugged into a vitamin drip, with a nurse like a bird of prey at his bedside, Athman is a pitiful sight. When he sees me, a redeeming smile splits his face.

"How goes it with the escape artist?"

He stirs among his dressings, breathing noisily. I beg him to stay calm and sit down, half-on and half-off the bed.

"You look like a grilled sausage wrapped up in toilet paper," I confide.

"Less of that. Help me sit up, instead."

I prop up his pillow with the care of a bomb-squad expert handling a mine. He thanks me with a nod.

The nurse finishes her tinkering and leaves us alone, man to man.

I look at the room: its walls are daubed a hideous gray, the bedside table soiled with the remnants of a pauper's meal.

"Nobody's brought you any flowers."

"It's not my funeral yet."

"Assassination attempt?"

"Accident."

"How did it happen?"

"An exposed cable. My workshop went up like a bale of hay. I didn't have time to escape."

"You could have said it was an assassination attempt. That would have increased your prestige, and afterward, you'd have the right to martyr status."

"I thought about it, but I was afraid of giving ideas to my former yes-men."

Athman and I have known each other since the seventies. We used to fight for the FLN*; I out of nationalism, he out of greed. He was a heartthrob of the Algerine Olympus, and he collected favors the way an old whore collects condoms.

He sighs.

"You've come here to feast your eyes on my misfortunes."

"I've told you before: good never comes of evil. But other people's bad luck isn't my bag, since you mention it."

He turns away.

Through the window veiled behind a curtain of cobwebs can be seen the mist enveloping the tops of the buildings with their ugly black hoods. Nerves exposed, the clouds create short circuits as they crash into each other. A light rain drums on the paving stones. It's not even six p.m., and in Algiers it's already night.

"What do you want, Llob?"

I toss the photo of Beelzebub onto his chest.

"Do you recognize him?"

"Of course. It's Alla Tej. He used to be my gardener. What's he done now?"

---

* *Translator's note*—FLN stands for *Front de Libération Nationale*, the National Liberation Front, founded in 1950s, to fight French colonialism

"Him? I don't know. I'm after his brother-in-law, Gaïd the Hairdresser."

"What's all this got to do with me?"

"You were his employer for years. You must know his habits. There must be somewhere I can get hold of him."

Athman moves painfully. His mulberry-colored face cracks in a mass of wrinkles. He grumbles, "I thought you'd come because of my accident."

"Some other time," I say mischievously. "For the moment, your servant has priority. It's important."

He lowers his head sadly. I let him ponder for a couple of seconds and then shake him again.

He gives in. "He hangs about over in Riad El-Feth. The address is 'Men's Toilets.'"

Upon which he turns toward the window and refuses to watch me leave.

In the corridor, I come upon Lino telling his life story to a nurse. I break in and ask, "Do we have anyone in Riad El-Feth?"

Lino puts his hands to his head like a biologist faced with some bizarre genetic mutation; he thinks, then snaps his fingers. "We've got Jo, boss."

※

Jo agreed to meet at Grill 69, in Riad El-Feth. It's a high-class joint with bay windows, mirrored ceilings, and red and white furnishings. The service is hushed and the customers single. Wafts of same-old-same-old and the odor of wealth politely compete with the establishment's air-conditioning, while languid music sets the crystal chandeliers tinkling. A few fairies mince about, batting their eyes, asses active beneath tight jeans. Here and there, schoolkid couples gaze at each other, one hand around a glass and the other under the table.

Our entrance raised a few eyebrows for a fraction of a second, after which we were ignored; Lino and I install ourselves near the door and now we're stuffing ourselves with a simple dish of grilled kidneys dotted with mustard. Free. The owner doesn't look like an angel, so he's making an investment. Since there's no risk of the specter of a bill spoiling the pleasure of dessert, Lino is abusing his hospitality. The owner keeps smiling, needless to say, but I think he's lost his faith. We won't catch him being the soul of charity to the starving again.

Ewegh occupies a table at the back, near the toilets. The proximity of an active pair of buttocks doesn't bother him at all. He surveys the room, weapon in hand.

"Nice place," says Lino, licking the dripping juice off his fingers. "One of these days I'll have to bring my little redhead here."

"I thought she was a blonde."

"Er…recent conquest. I'm an animal, you know."

"I didn't know."

"Well, now you do."

I wipe my mouth to hide a grin. The last time four-eyes went out with a girl was on a school outing. With the fire plug he has for a face, it's as much as he can do to be in the same room as his reflection. He strips the meat off a skewer, soaks it in mayonnaise, then *harissa*, then mustard—note the fluidity and judiciousness of the progression—and starts nibbling away, moaning with pleasure.

"What do you think, Super?"

"About what?"

"This place. My girl's going to love it."

"If you like getting ripped off."

"Er, I don't see anyone getting ripped off here."

Jo arrives at around 12:45, just as our benefactor is starting to go gray. I don't recognize her because of her disguise. She has chosen to practice the oldest profession Iranian-style: she wears a chador, with nothing underneath. It's ingenious and discreet, and protects against the evil eye.

She gives Lino a hug, kisses me respectfully on the top of my head, and sits down opposite us. The wear and tear of her profession has taken its toll on her small face. She has a beauty spot tattooed on her cheekbone, but the trace of an encounter that must have gone wrong can still be seen in a dark mark on her chin.

"It's been ages, Uncle Brahim," she exclaims, delighted.

"Hey, you've lost weight!"

"I watch my figure. How are Mina and the kids?"

"As usual. And you?"

"I have my ups and downs."

"Mmm. You're getting me all excited," yelps Lino.

She laughs, strokes his wrist affectionately, and says confidingly, "Your ponytail's great."

"What ponytail?"

What an asshole!

When I first knew Jo—real name Joher—she was a manager in a big state-owned enterprise. She was the perfect lady: severe haircut, square glasses. At the time, with her university baggage, she reckoned on having a good career. Except that in a phallocentric society, her only route to promotion was via her bed. Eventually she opened her legs—which is the equivalent, in the male of the species, of putting your hands up. A line formed straight away: from the director to the department head, from the bookkeeper to the security guard. Demand rose and rose, to the point that Joher had to give out double helpings to three potential string-pullers in rotation, sometimes coming close to overdosing. Worn out and disillusioned, she was fired and thrown into the gutter, where the police subjected her to unimaginable indignities. Then, one evening, for the purpose of a honey-trap operation, she agreed to play the sacrificial lamb for me. Since then, she's been a kind of occasional snitch for us while we, for our part, turn a blind eye to her tax affairs.

"What's the problem, uncle? I really don't have the time. I have two customers waiting for me in the basement."

I show her the photo of Alla Tej. She turns it over and over, tugging her lips, then asks, "He wasn't in *Planet of the Apes,* by any chance?"

"Maybe. At the moment, he's got a bit part in a remake of *The Time Machine.*"

She tilts her head to the left and then to the right. "Can I see a picture of him without the beard?"

"He seems to have been born with it."

Jo makes a small grimace and concentrates on the putative features of the man. Her long, tapering finger rustles against the photo, unconsciously scratching at the beard as if to penetrate its secret.

"I'm not sure, but I think I've seen him around."

"His name is Alla Tej. He takes sanctuary in these parts, especially the men's toilets, if you get my drift. We don't really know how deeply he's into terrorism, but he's not the type to cross his arms politely if he sees a coin on the ground. I need to have him to be sure. It's important."

Jo checks her watch nervously and puts the photo in her bag. She catches sight of Ewegh. The Tuareg's build makes her quiver from head to foot.

"He doesn't have the money," Lino warns her jealously.

"He's got other endowments, though."

She stands up, kisses my forehead, tugs the lieutenant's ponytail, and murmurs, "If that's the best you can do, well...there's not much hope."

Upon which she says goodbye and runs back to her transient lovers in the basement.

Chapter six

Thunder crashes with all its strength during the night. Every now and again blinding flashes of lightning bounce off the lower quarter, populating the nooks and crannies with nightmarish visions. It is ten o'clock, and not so much as a cat appears to have the guts to be out in the street.

For the last thirty-odd minutes, we've been at the top end of an old landing stage, watching an area that has every appearance of being a den of thieves as it sprawls endlessly toward the Bab el-Oued in an avalanche of caved-in roofs and poverty-stricken terraces. Except for an all-night shop, the blackout is total. The wind whistles lugubriously through the gaps in the city wall, mocking the unsecured windows, whose squeaking fills the silence with psychedelic symphonies.

The house we're interested in is at the base of the landing stage, next to a streetlight buried up to its neck under a small mountain of garbage. It's a low-slung shack, swathed in tattered layers of white-wash—a spine-chilling place.

Lino is panicking. "It'll be curfew soon. We'd best go in and find him."

"That's what I think too," says Jo in support from the backseat.

"I have a feeling he won't be getting any visitors tonight. A while ago he was drunk as a skunk. He's snoring by now for sure."

I nod, slip a flashlight into my coat pocket, and ready my nine-millimeter. "Okay, let's go."

"There's an exit at the back," adds Jo. "It opens onto an empty lot. If he tries to get away, we can catch him there."

The door trembles as Ewegh hurriedly skirts round a cluster of hovels to take up a position on the lot side.

I ask Jo to stay in the car and warn us in case of danger, then I go on ahead of Lino, who's too busy checking his magazine. A dog starts howling nearby.

As I pass, the shopkeeper pales under his walrus moustache. His eyebrows almost disappear at the sight of my piece. As if by levitation, his arms rise slowly in the air, his Adam's apple bobbing up and down in his throat. Lino gestures to him to sit down and zip it. The poor bastard brings his arms down slowly and disappears behind the racks of candy.

Gathering up all the guts and grit at my disposal, I move stealthily toward the door, make out the vague shape of a knocker and use it. It makes such a racket that the dog starts barking wildly. After the tenth knock, a sleepy voice asks, "Who's there?"

"Father Christmas."

"It's not December yet."

"December's for Christians. For Muslims it's Christmas all year round."

The voice coughs and then starts up again, even more irritably, "Just a minute, I'll get my keys."

Two minutes later, the door creaks horribly and Ewegh appears. Gesturing with his thumb, he explains, "He tried to make a run for it. I intercepted him."

"I hope you didn't kill him."

"I didn't check."

He leads us across a courtyard furrowed with foul-smelling culverts. An old van occupies what was once, a very long time ago, a garage. With his arms crossed and his face in the mud, Alla Tej is laid out in a vegetable garden, bound on four sides by unkempt trees. He doesn't regain consciousness until long after we carry him into a mildewed room.

When he comes to, he notices there's a tooth missing from his grimace. He stares at his bloodied hand and whines, "What the hell did you hit me with, a tire iron?"

Tej is plump and short-legged. His ragged mop of hair, the bristles poking out of his shirt, and his furry arms and his beard combine to make him look like a yak that has foreshortened its spine by trying to stand on its hind legs like a horse.

"You were trying to give us the slip," I remind him, as if he had lost the thread in the middle of a story.

He wipes his smashed lip on a scrap of curtain and shakes his head. His gaze comes to rest on the bulk of the Tuareg and then on his fists. Lino can be heard ransacking the room next door amid the sound of furniture being moved about.

Alla turns toward the racket. "Is there someone in there?"

"Only Father Christmas," I reassure him. "What got into you, pal? Are you on the run?"

"I thought you were Bosco's men."

"Who's this Bosco? A yeti-hunter?"

"My business partner. I owe him some cash. It's not my fault if I can't get the deal off the ground. The economy's in crisis, but Bosco doesn't want to know. And I'm not going to start mugging people in the street to pay him back."

"You're right. To begin with, you mug people because you have to, then you get a taste for it and it becomes a habit. That's not good."

"Look what I found in his hidey-hole, Super," Lino says exult-antly, brandishing a chunk of hashish.

"It's not mine," Tej protests, standing up.

Ewegh seizes him by the shoulders and plants him back down in the chair. Tej protests again. With disdain, I lift his chin with my finger and say, "Listen, asshole. If you start suggesting we put that muck in your house to make trouble for you, I'll stop thinking you're incapable of mugging people in the street. We know you're a dealer, that you bought yourself a nice F-5, a four-bedroom apartment, and that this is just a hideout where you strip stolen cars to feed the black market with spare parts, that your sister is married to a notorious terrorist, and that thick beard or no thick beard, you've got no more chance of ending up in paradise than a member of parliament."

Tej is reading my eyes and appears to find something there that reassures him. He guesses it's not in his interest to turn down the chance I'm about to give him.

"What do you want from me?"

"I've got a deal for you."

"This bank's gone bust."

Lino swings his foot. The yak recoils. His chair tips over and he ends up sprawled against the bed frame. Ewegh picks him up and dumps him back on the chair.

"I'm not going to say it twice," I warn him. "Either you talk or we have some fun. We can't afford both. What's it going to be?"

Tej stares at Lino and sees the jaws of a carnivore, then lowers his head to make us believe he's capable of thinking.

"Well?"

"We'll talk."

"Great. We'll pretend you've just been born again. I grant you absolution. In return, you carry a message to your brother-in-law Ali Gaïd."

"I don't know where he is, I swear. Ali hasn't set foot in the family since the business with the derailed train."

I ask Lino, "Do you believe him?"

"Not really."

"What about you, Ewegh?"

Ewegh shakes his head.

I spread my arms in a gesture of regret. "Think of something else, asshole. If my deal doesn't interest you, I'll offer it to someone else. And as your reward you'll be first in line for the scrap heap."

He scratches the bridge of his nose. A thread of reddish saliva dribbles from the corner of his mouth.

"What's your deal?"

"Gaïd Ali's holding on to something that doesn't belong to him. I want to get it back."

"What is it?"

"It's a diskette. He lifted it from the house of a friend of mine at place de la Charité. My friend has completely lost his head over it."

"I don't know what you're talking about."

"You don't have to. Just give him the message. Your brother-in-law will understand. Tell him I don't give a damn about his being a fugitive. I just want the diskette."

"And after I've run your errand I can go home without having you on my ass?"

"We're not suppositories."

He behaves as though he's not very enthusiastic. Ewegh grabs him by the scruff of his neck and lifts him up.

"My name is Ewegh Seddig. I'm color-blind. I can't tell the difference between a funeral shroud and a white flag, so I don't take prisoners. There aren't thirty-six solutions. Either you carry this thing through to the end, or it's all over for you."

Alla calms him with both hands.

"Take it easy, crusher, you're messing up my shirt. I'll see what I can do."

"And don't even think of double-crossing us," Lino growls.

⋇

What didn't work with Ben Hamid the barman seems to do the trick with Alla Tej. Two minutes after we left, our Beelzebub went to the shop to make a phone call. They must have said they'd call him back, because he sat on the counter and ordered the grocer to get lost. The telephone rings three times. Alla doesn't react. One minute later, he picks up on the first ring. After the conversation, he goes back to the shack, changes his clothes, and starts waiting in front of the entrance.

At about eleven, a Renault arrives with its headlights off, goes around the square once, and comes back to pick him up. We start our engine and follow at a distance.

About a mile down the hill, the Renault avoids a police road block and disappears into a suburb whose blackness has even sucked up the sickly light of the streetlamps. We search for it across a building site spiky with girders and cranes and catch up with it beside a square of magnificent, brand-new mansions.

Alla Tej and his driver stay inside the vehicle, under a mimosa tree, for a good quarter of an hour before they decide to set foot outside. They walk down two alleys and go into a villa without announcing themselves.

We wait for an eternity. This time, seeing nothing happening, I decide to go and find out what's going on. Ewegh goes off down a neighboring street on his own, like a grown-up. Lino and I walk up to the villa. The grilled gate is ajar. A marbled path leads us to a solid oak door, also open. I switch on my flashlight and venture into the interior of the dwelling.

We go over the bedrooms, the bathroom, the laundry, and the wardrobes with a fine-tooth comb. The two villains have evaporated.

"There's a swimming pool in the garden," Ewegh tells me, empty-handed. "They must have escaped that way."

We retrace our steps.

Just as we get to the grilled gate, the sky falls in on us.

"Police!" someone shouts. "Hands on your heads, and don't move!"

"Don't shoot," begs Lino with a catch in his voice. "We're cops too."

"Son of a bitch!" cries Lieutenant Chater as he appears from behind a paddy wagon "What the fuck are you doing here? We nearly took you out."

"My retina's coming detached," I shout at him, literally blinded by the searchlights.

Lieutenant Chater orders his men to put the safety screen back on. Since I can't see anything, he slips his hand under my armpit and helps me walk.

"We got an anonymous phone call telling us there were three suspicious-looking men, armed, at 16, rue Bahia Dahro. Just as well that Lino shouted, or we'd have taken you for terrorists."

I say to Lino, "So the yak was no donkey."

"No, in fact he's made jackasses out of us."

44

The Renault has disappeared.

As for Jo, who had stayed in the car, all we found was a shoe and a lipstick on the road.

The next day, at eight o'clock on the dot, Alla Tej doesn't even give me time to take off my coat. His laugh booms on the other end of the line. "So which of us is the asshole, Llob? If I made sure you're still alive, it was just so you'd know I could."

"Where's Jo?"

"You mean the whore? She's at 16, rue Bahia Dahro. Exactly where your buddies nearly did you in, all three of you. And another thing, *asshole:* tell your crazy dinosaur that we don't give gifts or take prisoners either."

⁂

The sky is a dazzling blue. After yesterday's downpours, the green of the foliage is so brilliant it seems freshly painted. Birds trill in the unmoving trees. It really is a picture of tranquility. On the deckchair beside the pool, shaded by an umbrella that wasn't there yesterday, Jo appears to be dreaming…But what kind of a dream can you have when your throat has been slit from ear to ear?

I grab a branch to withstand the blow.

The devil can finally retire; the succession is assured.

Chapter seven

Alla Tej must have finally realized that if beards had anything going for them at all, they wouldn't grow out of people's asses.

Clean shaven, with gel in his hair, he looks ten years younger. An imperceptible thread of mascara accentuates his eyes and brings unexpected freshness to his drag-queen features. I don't know how he managed to squeeze inside his jeans, which are about the right size for a scarecrow but which show the shape of his backside better than any topographical map; I don't know whether his own mother would recognize him among the young people gyrating frantically on the dance floor at the Djinn Rouge cabaret. For my part, I quickly zeroed in on him amid the frenzied decibels and flashing lights, thanks to his distinctive aura of damnation.

I'm leaning on my elbows at the bar, a glass of orange juice in my mitts, watching the beautiful people in the mirror in front of me. I've been resisting the advances of kooks and druggies for quite a while. Suddenly, Alla Tej emerges from the herd. His vile, feral stare collides with mine. He flees instantly, parting the crowd before him.

I don't even give chase.

He runs up the stairs four at a time, ends up on a balcony, gives me a one-armed salute, and disappears down a corridor.

I calmly adjust my tunic. I'm relaxed.

A rancid whore sandwiched between youth and old age invades my space with her tits.

"I'm gay," I tell her, to put her off.

With my customary politeness, I apologize to left and right as I clear a path to the balcony. At the top of the staircase, the corridor starts by tying itself in knots, then breaks its neck as it goes on into another landing. A French window gives onto a garden decorated with miniature lanterns. In a sky studded with millions of pearls, the gods count the clouds and hum a tune. It's a fine night to catch yourself a son of a bitch.

It's obvious that Ewegh has brought his left arm into action, because Alla Tej is on the ground, the right side of his face completely caved in. He's crawling along, gasping; he hangs onto a radiator but can't manage to get up.

I've been chasing him for three weeks. I've mobilized my best sleuths and my best snitches to track him down. The proof that Our Lord lives—well, there it is, groggy, on all fours!

I brace myself and shoot him in the kidneys. Alla rolls over twice and ends up against the wall, his mouth open for a scream that won't come out.

I grab him by the hair, hard enough to crack his skull.

"Thanks for standing me up, darling. We must get together again when I retire."

We drag him into the toilets at the end of the hallway and close the door behind us.

Alla curls himself around his kidneys, moaning. His hand slips furtively down toward his ankle and a knife hidden under his sock. My .45 goes off and dislocates his shoulder on the spot. To stop him, stirring up the whole neighborhood, Ewegh grabs him by the neck and belt, sticks his head in the toilet, and flushes.

"That'll clear his head."

Alla collapses on the floor and throws up in his own lap.

I place the point of the knife on his nose, follow its outline, touch the tip of his chin, tickle his Adam's apple.

"This is the contaminated piece of scrap metal you used to slit Jo's throat."

"Go to the devil!"

"He sent me. I'm going to bleed you dry, you piece of shit!"

He looks at me disdainfully and spits bloody saliva in my face.

"Fuck you, you barnyard pig! You're just a fanatic and an asshole."

He contines the insult by offering up his throat.

"Go ahead, slit my throat. Chicken! Try to slit it! Afraid you'll faint?"

I wipe my face with a handkerchief. My hand isn't shaking. I'm calm.

I address Big Chief Standing Yak: "I've got an idea. Let's play Arabian Nights, okay? You be Scheherazade and I'll be the sultan. You can tell me all about your little pals, their hideouts, their plans. Ewegh, over there, he can be Damocles. If you stop talking, he'll hit you over the head until your brains start leaking out of your nostrils. If you survive, you earn a reprieve until tomorrow night. What do you think?"

He prepares a load in his throat with which to express his contempt. This time, my hand gets there first. I wring his neck and make him swallow his bile.

Like trained monkeys—great as a chorus but lousy soloists—Standing Yak cracks after a few slaps. Not because my methods are persuasive but because God's little undesirables are masters of the about-face. They turn their coats so quickly there's hardly any skin left on their backs.

❧

The hideout Alla Tej has led to is on the first floor of a hotel on rue Safir Barlach, the kind where you rent rooms by the hour. The area is overcrowded. It smells of potholes and sweat for miles around.

Here, standing shoulder to shoulder has as much to do with staying upright as expressing solidarity. Drop a needle from a balcony and it won't reach the ground. Besides, there's so much laundry hanging over the street that old men have trouble finding a spot of sunlight to put their stools out in.

The hotel loiters in a cul-de-sac. Maybe it gets laid there. Veiled whores drift in and out, offering a good time, pretending to be fortune-tellers so as not to outrage any sensitivities. Two down-and-outs sit on the curb, one eye on the herd and the other staring into space. A few customers circle the merchandise guiltily, ready to make a hasty retreat should a familiar face appear in the vicinity.

Lino gives us the thumbs-up from the terrace of an unsavory looking café. He has bunched his ponytail up under a fez and put on a robe so as to blend into the scenery; nevertheless, his cop aura marks him out like an sign of damnation.

Ewegh goes in first, checks the ground floor of the place, and comes back to cover me from the door. I push Standing Yak over to the reception desk. The strapping individual at the till is huge as sin. Hind feet on the counter, chair leaning against the wall, he's reading a comic book called *Slim* and laughing silently.

"One room free in the basement," he announces without closing his comic. "Five notes for twenty minutes. No haggling here. We save our breath for when it counts."

Finally he deigns to look up and switches from Alla to me, as if to change the subject.

"And I'm doing you a favor at that. This isn't an old people's home. We don't accept retirees around here."

"Really? Why ever not?" I ask him.

"Are you kidding? At your age you've already got one foot in the grave."

"Even if I had both feet there I'd still have a third to kick your ass, hippo!"

I sweep his dreadlocks aside irritably and shove my *taghout* card in his face. "The key to room 13, and show us the way."

I saw a few pigsties when I was working for the Juliens as their gofer, but room 13 deserves a special mention in the *Guinness Book*. There's such a stench that I'm afraid of setting off an explosion when I press the buzzer.

"Who does the housekeeping?"

"The tenant."

"Does he rent by the month, this guy?"

"He's paid for a quarter, but he's seldom there."

I show him the picture of Sid Ahmed Merouan, a.k.a. TNT.

"Hey, that's him!"

"Did he live alone?"

"With a girl."

"Where can we find her?"

"I don't know."

"Is she one of the house girls?"

"Not one of ours. She's got a wart on her nose, which she calls a beauty spot. You can't miss her: size of a farmhouse dresser, with a red wig on top and a pair of false eyelashes that'll take your eye out at the first kiss."

"Do you know who she is?" I ask Standing Yak.

"Her name's Brigitte."

"French?"

"Not really. She's called that because she looks like a ship with that name."

I ask the receptionist to go back to his cage, and start rifling through the mess. Shoes covered with mildew, disgusting clothes, busted revolver, do-it-yourself bomb-making manuals, stick of dynamite. In a drawer I come upon a cardboard file folder. Inside, I find photos of Athman Mamar, his dog and his house, and a plan of his workshop.

While my back is turned, Alla Tej takes to his heels down the corridor. This doesn't distract me for one moment. The sound of running stops abruptly and is followed by the sound of a fall.

"I hope you didn't kill him," I grumble as I carry on searching under the bed.

"I didn't check," says Ewegh from the end of the corridor.

One thing's for sure: if Alla Tej insists on trying to give us the slip like this, before long his face will be so flat you'll be able to iron your shirt on it.

Chapter eight

Athman Mamar is temporarily sitting in his wheelchair by
the window, his limbs painted with disinfectant and his face swollen
with sores. He's soaking up the sunlight, oblivious as a hermit. He
doesn't turn around when he hears the door of his room opening.

"Hi, Rameses. I've brought you some sweeties from Paris."

I put the bag of candy on the bedside table and lay a sympa-
thetic hand on his shoulder, making him start with pain.

"Sorry."

"That's okay. I'm getting used to my shirt of Nessus."

"Who's he, a fireman?"

He spins his chair around to show me his face, a study in
purple fit to make your hair stand on end.

"The nurse finds a map of the world in my features," he says
self-pityingly.

"She's too kind."

His mocking smile cracks and his hands clasp his knees, the
knuckles milky white.

I extract the file from beneath my jacket and lay it out on
the bed.

"I found this in the home of a bomb-maker whom we can thank for most of the bombings that have taken place in the capital. One Sid Ahmed Merouan, a.k.a. TNT."

Athman turns his head with difficulty and looks; he recognizes the plan of his workshop and leans back on his cushion.

"What exactly do you want, Llob?"

"You lied to me. The fire in your workshop wasn't caused by a short circuit."

"It's not your problem. I'm a big boy now: I can wipe my own ass."

I pick up the plan, fold it carefully, and put it back in the inside pocket of my jacket.

"I had a conversation with your other half this morning. She's not looking so hot, I must say. She says you've had a lot of phone calls recently, that you weren't exactly ecstatic when you hung up, and that you spent most of your time sniffing the window curtains. Who are you afraid of?"

He just stares at the tiles. I position myself between him and the light. My opacity annoys him. He turns onto his side to look at the buildings in the street.

"She remembers Ben Ouda, too. He was a pal of yours."

"In those days I had pals coming out of my ears."

"I see. The last time he came to see you, he was in quite a state."

"He'd just gone bankrupt. Not surprising he wasn't happy."

"Your other half says Dahman Faïd, the billionnaire, ordered you not to bail the dip out. Is it because you disobeyed orders that you started getting phone calls?"

"I'm nobody's keeper."

"Why did Faïd want to keep Ben Ouda on the ropes?"

"You'd better ask him."

"Do you know that your gardener, Alla Tej, was spying on you for the billionnaire?"

"I was paying him to look after my garden."

"You don't seem surprised."

"So now you *know* I'm a big boy."

"He's playing Scheherazade with me every night. He's told me a few things. For example, after the murder of Ben Ouda, Professor Nasser Abad came to see you."

"So what? He was my wife's brother."

"Oh?"

This is getting interesting. I rest my honorable posterior on the bed, putting a pillow under my thigh because of the slight tension.

Athman Mamar wheels his barrow back against the wall and studies me with an evil look in his eye.

I light a cigarette.

"Strange all the same, don't you think, this chain reaction? Ben Ouda decapitated a week after he visits you. Then the prof. Then your workshop up in flames, with you in it. Then the blood-sucking influence of this Faïd. And Alla, just about everywhere. Two and two makes four: either you're jinxing your mates or you're in the shit with them."

"You've been a cop too many years, Llob."

"This time I have a feeling this has nothing to do with Pavlov. I've checked my files. Everything leads me to believe I've put my finger on something significant."

"If you want my advice, don't let it hang about there too long. Else you won't be able to suck it later."

"I've got nine spares."

"They're not enough."

I breathe the smoke out over my fingernails and say, "Do you know why horses mark their route with fat turds?"

"No."

"Because they can't stand diapers."

"I don't follow you."

"That shows I'm on your tail."

I look him right in the eye to stop him turning away.

"What's going on, Athman?"

He scratches the back of his hand nervously, takes off some skin and doesn't notice. After a long silence, his expression lights up and he says, "Envious people are trying to put a brake on my commercial success. As the market opens up, the floodgates give way. If you haven't got a proper mooring you'll be swept away in the flood. Everyone's trying to clear some space up around them to gain a bit of breathing space. That's the investment battle. You torpedo each other hard, but all's fair."

"Do you really expect me to believe this rubbish?"

"At least I'll have tried my luck."

I get out the notebook I borrowed from Lino, pretend to check my notes, and stop on a page that is as blank as it is distressing and random.

"Ben Ouda and the prof knew each other through you."

"At my house, yes; through me, no. They had many things in common."

"For example?"

"Boys and books."

"That's what my notebook says too. They got on like a house on fire, apparently."

"They listened to each other talk, rather."

"Supposing you tell me about H-I-V," I say suddenly.

"H.I. who?"

Missed!

I nod. A truck roars in the street, reawakening my fury.

"It's time for your injection, Mister Mamar," the nurse thunders as she jostles me on her way in.

"I haven't finished with him."

"I don't give a damn. This is a clinic, not a mental hospital. I must ask you to leave now. My patient needs to rest."

I try to frown.

She pulls her lips back in a cannibalistic leer.

"Now, Superintendent!"

"Go away," the mummy adds. "You're making me itch again."

Persuaded, I put my finger to the corner of my forehead in a casual salute and beat a retreat.

From the corridor, I hear the nurse, annoyed:

"Does he think he can terrorize us with his shitty little badge, or what?"

To which Athman replies, "Forget that asshole, and give me another little treat like yesterday, only this time try to keep your hands behind your back."

Chapter nine

Dahman Faïd came into the world with the sole purpose of amassing cash. As a baby—or so his official biography would have it—his crying sounded like the whirring of a one-armed bandit. There was no question of his accepting his bottle unless you slipped a bank note under his bib. Extortion, prostitution, drugs, smuggling, politics—there isn't a racket he isn't involved in.

The only place he's never invested in is the paradise of Allah. He has no illusions on that score.

His building rises up as you come out of Hydra, monumental as an obelisk erected to the spirits of troubled waters. Seven floors of picture windows, frontage lush with greedy plants, a sumptuous lobby that fondly recalls an imperial railway station.

Lino cuts a swathe through the morning crowd besieging the counters. The more people turn to look as he goes by, the more he shakes his ponytail from side to side.

"Think they're impressed by my hairstyle, Super?"

"You bet!"

"Next time," he promises with absurd seriousness, "I'll wear a helmet."

I'm racked with the desire to explain the facts of life to him, but as a man who is aware of the mental shipwreck of a fellow human being, I let it pass. No one is more deaf than a self-deluded sucker.

A carrottop the size of a pair of mules intercepts us at reception. He raises his arm to show us he's carrying a gun.

"We're police officers," I say in an attempt to intimidate him.

"Nobody's perfect," he retorts.

"Superintendent Llob. Your redeemer's expecting me."

Immediately, he becomes rigid with obsequiousness and invites me to follow him to an elevator that's so sophisticated you feel like renting it for the day.

Before dispatching me toward the heavens he frisks me; he jumps when his hand strikes the butt of my nine-millimeter.

"You're armed, Superintendent?"

"Only with a prosthesis."

Embarrassed, he uses the telephone on the wall and negotiates with the handset.

"It's all right," he says, hanging up. "You can keep it."

Lino doesn't even have time to tidy up his ponytail before Carrottop puts him to one side as if separating wheat from chaff.

"One at a time. You, sperm cell, try not to make a mess on the carpet in the lounge over there while you wait for your egg cell to come back."

Lino waits for me to blow my top on his behalf. I spread my arms apologetically and allow myself to be swallowed up by the elevator.

The bimbo that greets me halfway to heaven is as lovely as can be. The supermodel type: a dipstick like Lino would gladly give ten years of his life for the chance to flaunt her on his arm for two minutes. A fiery mane and clear eyes: she has those, as well as a multiskilled mouth and an extremely liberated chest.

"Has he got the wrong trough?" I ask her.

"Who, sir?"

"That sweet little piglet stuck in your cleavage."

She giggles and offers to take my coat. I refuse politely on account of the holes in my jacket.

Like Pharoah at the peak of his empire, Dahman Faïd is loung-ing at the end of his unwelcoming office, a cigar in his mouth and the world at his feet. He is huge and bald, with porcupine quills all over his hypocrite's face, and he's telling some amber beads. The click-ing of the beads is like a deadly tick-tock in the midst of the silence, matching my pulse and making my mouth dry up.

He hurries to divert me toward a chair so as not to have to shake my hand. "Take a seat, Columbo."

I fall into an armchair so soft I feel as though I'm flat on my back.

"I'll give you three minutes," he fires at me. "My schedule is packed."

His harshness awakens the menial within. My heart starts playing tricks on me, and acid secretions start to ferment in my guts. Like anyone who knows the way things work, I have of course been dreading this encounter. I now realize that even with my ingrained pessimism I was a long way short of the mark.

"It's about Ben Ouda," I say, without beating around the bush.

"I thought he was dead and buried."

"That's right, and I'm inquiring into his premature death, Mister Faïd. The deceased was a friend of yours."

"That word is quite a pejorative one, in the vocabulary of the stock exchange," he interjects, blowing smoke in my direction.

"Duly noted, sir. What proportion of your turnover did he represent, exactly?"

He doesn't appreciate the new phrasing of my question. His left cheek trembles. He must think I prepared my script.

"Not much."

"Meaning?"

He checks his watch. Ostentatiously.

"He was quite rich. I invested his cash for a fee."

"It seems you parted stormily."

"It's not unusual in mercenary relationships. Ben was making a play for the whole pie and refused to understand that his dentures weren't up to the job. He went bankrupt. He wanted to become a financial virgin again. I don't lend to vestals. He slammed the door and left."

I say "hmm" to bring my racing pulse under control, and then take a chance: "Did you know he was putting together a book?"

"I'm not a publisher."

"He didn't talk to you about it?"

"The only books I care about are the account books, Columbo."

"I have reason to believe that's why he was killed."

"Think what you like."

His thick lips gather themselves around his cigar. I try to hold his gaze but don't manage. Dahman Faïd is worth several billion. He is capable of overturning the Republic with a single sneeze. His pockets are stuffed with members of parliament, and the authorities eat out of the palm of his hand. During the heyday of one-party government, he had the right of veto over government programs and felt free to remove magistrates and civil servants without fear of objections. Any candidate, and it didn't matter what field he was in, who didn't benefit from his *baraka* had no more chance of being retained than a course of civics handed out to a vandal.

To the best of my knowledge, his totalitarian control has never been breached.

"Seriously," he belches, as he taps on his cigar, "what makes you think Ben's death has anything to do with his book? He's written plenty of them, each one as twisted as the last, and nobody pays any attention. People are hungry, Columbo. They're trying to drag themselves up out of the shit, not make their lives complicated with foolish theories. Ben liked pretty boys. He spent more time chasing ass than paying attention to the company he kept. His harem was packed with drug addicts, screw-ups, losers, and psychopaths. Personally, I've never for one moment connected his demise with the cultural purge that's raging through the country. If you want some advice, look in a few illicit basements. You'd be more at home."

"His killers have been identified."

"What's stopping you from bringing them in?"

"That's what I intend to do."

"In that case, what are you doing in my house?"

I examine him: sperm-whale jaws, bird-of-prey claws, hyena laugh—he's a veritable menagerie, all in one person.

"You've got thirty seconds left, Columbo."

"Would you mind calling me Superintendent?"

"I can call you Pope, if you like. It's all the same to me."

I nod.

"I suppose I'm wasting my time, Mister Faïd."

"Mine, mainly."

❧

I haven't stopped ruminating the whole day, and I still can't digest the stodgy outrage committed by Dahman Faïd upon me, representative of public order in the exercise of his duty that I am.

At one point I even considered returning to the site of the affront to give the oaf a good beating. And where would that have gotten me? In a land where the law instinctively prostitutes itself to large fortunes, I would only succeed in unleashing the thunderbolts of the Administration.

Then, like every time I am brought face to face with my disappointments, which are those of a fool from which every last thing has been confiscated, I thought about handing in my badge and going back to Mina and the kids, to where my brother has been hiding them for six months as a security measure.

I can go on repeating to myself that the courageous must not let themselves be beaten down, that the fate of a nation depends on their obstinately holding out against the omnipotent hydra-headed monster; I can go on dreaming of a day when justice will finally triumph over influence-peddling and favoritism; I can go on believing that, in a sky studded with billions of stars, there's one for me, more beautiful than all the galaxies combined; but in the end the self-confidence flaunted by the Dahman Faïds of this world never fails to drain my vitality.

I ask Lino to take me for a drive along the coast road. The

Mediterranean has inestimable therapeutic properties, but even Barbarossa* would have been driven up the wall by the lieutenant's exasperating chatter.

In the end, afraid that a stroke might floor me beyond the next bend, I ask my colleague to let me take the wheel and then get lost.

"How do I get back?" Lino protests from the pavement.

"On foot."

"This is an unsavoury neighborhood, Super."

"Okay, so you'll get back feet first."

Upon which I put my foot to the floor without turning around.

On the sun-glazed road, I see *fellahin* breaking their backs in their fields, truck drivers hugging the steering wheel with their arms, women waiting for a forgetful bus, children jogging to school, idlers meditating on the terraces of cafés, old men rotting against fences. On their faces, despite the burden of uncertainty and the darkness of the nation's drama, I glimpse a wondrous kind of serenity—the faith of an easy-going people, generous to the point of handing over their last shirt, so humble they arouse the contempt of those who have not understood a word of the prophets. And just because of their gaze, just because of their long suffering, verging on fatalism, just because of their dignity that is still perceptible through the opacity of misfortune, I swipe dangerously at the steering wheel, right in the middle of the road, and speed back along the coast road to fetch Lino.

* A notorious sixteenth-century Barbary pirate who sailed the Mediterranean, whose real name was Baba Arrouj. The French corrupted his name into Barbarossa.

Part II

Chapter ten

I turn up at 5, rue Mosbah, at one o'clock on the dot, Sid Ali's sandwich like an anvil in my belly. Feral kids scatter in front of the hood of my car, boisterous and hysterical, knocked for six by the bloodbath that has just grafted itself onto their poverty.

Police cars block the twisting alleyway, and a swarm of Ninjas mount guard on the surrounding rooftops. The inescapable Bliss is waiting for me on the threshold of the terrace, his nose in a handkerchief.

"You'd be better off getting out your gas mask, Llob," he tells me in his nasal voice. "It stinks to high heaven in there."

"I wouldn't need it if you'd vacate the area."

"I'm no skunk."

"You're a menace to the ozone layer."

Lino snickers corrosively behind me.

Bliss chooses to let it go and moves aside to let us past.

We enter a small courtyard littered with rubble and other debris. Ben Hamid, the café owner, is hanging from a lemon tree, in his underwear. His wrists are bound and he has a thick cloth in his mouth. Beneath his charred feet, a heap of ashes tells us something of the difficult moments that marked his passage from life to death.

"The woman's inside," Lieutenant Chater informs me.

We go through a dilapidated living room where three camp beds are molding around a treacherous pedestal table. The floor is littered with newspapers and beer cans. To the right of a soot-streaked oil stove, a door leads to a nausea-inducing kitchen. Leftover food has gone moldy in the bottom of the dishes, and the glasses have repulsive stains.

The woman is in the bathroom, whose walls are spattered with blood. She is vast and naked. The skin has been torn off her back, and her throat has been slit from ear to ear.

My lunch stirs in my guts.

Bliss moistens his finger with the tip of his tongue and solemnly turns the pages of his notebook. "The relic in the courtyard, that's Ben Hamid. He was the manager of the Circle of Friends, a little café in the heart of the casbah. As for the woman, she was a prostitute. She went by the name of Brigitte."

The sergeant appears with a bony old man, billowy in a worn *gandoura*.

"This is the neighbor across the way."

The old man pushes his fez back, scratches his head, and looks sheepish.

"I mean, I didn't see the whole thing," he says hesitantly. "I'm not a peeping tom. I was at the window, waiting for the call of the muezzin."

"Nobody's saying anything against you."

That makes him feel better. He turns to the hanged man, whom the officers are trying to release, and says:

"He wasn't the most honest of men."

"What happened?"

"An ambulance stopped in front of the terrace. I thought Ben Hamid wasn't well. I was wrong."

He pauses for a moment to collect his thoughts, then carries on. "They didn't bring a stretcher out of the ambulance; it was Ben

Hamid and a woman of great bulk. They were pretty smashed up. Four men were laying into them."

"What time was it?"

"A bit before the *El-Icha* call."

"Eight o'clock," the sergeant explains.

"The ambulance left. All of a sudden a Mercedes turned up. Two guys got out. They were all dressed up, like the mannequins they put in shop windows on the boulevards."

"What were they like, these guys?"

"Ordinary."

"Meaning?"

"One of them was thin, with a moustache."

"And the other one?"

"Ordinary."

"Thin, with a moustache?"

"Oh no, he was tall as a billboard, with a shaved head and a pear-shaped earring in his left ear. The other one, the little one, screwed something onto his gun and shot out the light. I didn't see anything after that."

I lay a grateful hand on his shoulder. For him, it's as if his patron saint were blessing him. I feel as though I could hold him, all of him, in the palm of my hand.

"You didn't notice the number of the Mercedes?"

"I can't read."

"Thank you, *haj*, you've been very cooperative."

The sergeant grabs him by the elbow and drags him roughly toward the door.

؟؉

I haven't even had time to leave a fingerprint on my cup of coffee when the boss summons me to join him in his ivory tower. I find him standing in front of the window, fingers interlocked behind his back, contemplating the bay of Algiers. When I detect Bliss's presence, I understand that I haven't been called in for a medal.

I stand at attention for an eternity. Since no one seems to be noticing my sense of discipline, I cough into my fist to attract the director's attention. And it is his partner in crime that reacts: "Shh! He's thinking."

"Excuse me?"

Bliss makes himself smaller and repeats in a low voice. "The director is thinking."

In my turn, I lean on his shoulder and whisper, "How irritating. He'll use up his last remaining gram of brain, and then he won't be able to mess anything else up."

Bliss snickers, sensibly moving his rodent's face out of range of my breath.

"Your tongue will do you in one day, Llob."

"Less serious than the loss of your soul, Mephisto. What have you told him on my behalf? He seems mighty pissed off."

"He's still upset about Jo. It was tacky to leave her on her own."

My hand leaps to his throat.

"That's enough!" snaps the boss, pivoting round.

His face is pale. For an instant I think his false teeth are going to spring out of his mouth and bite me. Without moving away from the window, he flashes me a black look, and then, with an exasperated gesture, lets it pass.

"Your bickering makes me tired."

Bliss lowers his head contritely.

The chief sags into his throne, swivels it with a heave of his body, then eyes me lopsidedly.

"Did you read the daily bulletin this morning? A Comms team *worked out* where Merouan TNT's hideout was. The bastard had booby-trapped all the access points. They barely touched the handle of a window and the whole house went up. Result: three bomb-squad guys down and the best part of the street reduced to rubble."

He stands up, goes back to his viewing point, then comes back toward me.

"That makes three months you've been going round in circles, Superintendent. During that time, we've gone on burying our dead."

"I'm doing what I can."

"It's not enough."

"It's the best I can do with the resources I've been allocated."

His lips draw back in a snarl and his eyes blaze. "Your insinuations are ridiculous!"

Bliss is watching me intently through half-closed eyes. Knowing his skill with magic spells, he dares to say, "It's the way he's made, director. Every time he's in a tight corner he invents an emergency exit… Your problem, Llob, is that you lack proper technique. Gaïd's group isn't impossible to find, it's that you go about chasing them the wrong way. From the beginning I told the director you were looking for a needle in a haystack. With anyone else, I'd have intervened, but your excessive pride put me off."

"Do you know what I think of you, Bliss Nahs?"

He cuts me off with a raised finger, stands up slowly, straightens his tie, flattens the front of his jacket, and draws himself up on tiptoe. Unfortunately for him, his head doesn't reach past my belt buckle.

"I know what you think of me, and it's the least of all my worries."

He goes up to the director's desk and pushes a book in my direction. "This is probably one of the motives for the crime. Ben Ouda's last work, *Dream and Utopia*. I've read it twice. The director and I are convinced…"

"I've read it. You're not telling me anything I don't know already."

"I'm not the only one, alas!"

He opens the book at page five and places his finger on a dedication. "'Affectionately, to my friend Abderrahman Kaak,'" he reads. "Instead of running around right and left, why not try this trail?"

The director scribbles quickly on a piece of paper and hands it to me. "His address."

I look at the piece of paper, the book, the two scoundrels, apparently well pleased with their love affair, the bay through the window, my shoes, the ceiling—and nowhere can I find the space to insert a single word. I grab the piece of paper cheerfully and keep my chin up. No question of making a spectacle of myself. Nobility lies in not showing outrage when simple contempt will suffice.

⅍

Lino came to get me as usual. I let him honk his horn in the street. He took a while to realize that I had no desire to go to my office, that I wanted to be alone.

I spent the night wrestling with my pillow. All morning, worn out from lack of sleep, I've been unable to decide whether I should shave or flush myself down the toilet.

My mood is ratty enough for ten sewers.

Outside, the parboiled city is on edge. Dissonant throbbing is answered by ululating sirens. Spring has not finished packing its bags, and already Algiers reminds one of a barbecue suspended between God's hell and man's purgatory.

I'm suffocating.

Some days you want nothing to do with the universe; you want to tell the Republic to go to hell.

Finally, tired of staring at myself in the mirror like a moron, I jump in my Zastava and drive around long enough to make the radiator boil over. The heat makes me stop in front of a coffeehouse, and I tell myself wistfully that a nice cup of coffee might help order my thoughts. There are a lot of people in the room, which is hazy with tobacco smoke. Despite the best effort of four air conditioners, it feels like a *hammam*. A brotherhood of truants and head-in-the-clouds theoreticians is putting the world to rights or destroying it, as the whim takes them. There are hookers hanging about in the alcoves. Some of them are smoking, cheeks resting in their hands. Others are trying vainly to tempt their prey. Their weary gaze holds a singular gleam, the same gleam that distinguishes the reflection in a mirror from the spark in a serpent's eye.

I take up a position at the counter. Since chance does as it pleases in our country, I happen upon Captain Berrah. There he is, sitting on the stool beside me, staring thoughtfully ahead. Poor thing! His profile has no more relief than a plumb line. When, in turn, he notices me, he immediately looks around for Ewegh.

"I left him in his kennel," I reassure him.

"Just as well."

He smiles.

His ugly mug breaks my heart.

"Is this your day off?" I ask him.

"I'm waiting for someone."

I signal to the waiter. Instead of coming straight over, he turns his back ostentatiously.

"In this place you make like you're at home," the captain confides. "Tea or coffee?"

"Coffee."

He pulls a coffee pot over, fills a cup, and pushes it in my direction.

"You look like you've emerged from a dunghill, Superintendent. Problems?"

"Not really. Just constipation of the moral kind."

He offers me an American cigarette and holds out his lighter.

"And your investigation?"

"Not encouraging."

"Things aren't looking too good for us either. We were within a hairsbreadth of cornering Brahim Zaddam. Remember him? The Afghan veteran. He was involved in Ben Ouda's murder. Three days ago, an armed group snatched him from under our noses. Yesterday, we found his body in a rubbish dump. He'd been tortured long and hard before he croaked."

"I bet there was an ordinary-looking guy, tall as a billboard, with a shaved head and a pear on his ear, among the kidnappers."

The captain immediately stops fiddling with his lighter.

"Were you there?"

"No, but there's a bald guy on my team."

I nudge him with my elbow and say, "I'm asking myself questions and I can't fill in the blanks."

"Maybe you're holding the questionnaire upside down. We at Comms are sure a rival group is eliminating the Gaïd group."

I taste my coffee, find it's too sweet, and look around for a spittoon.

The captain checks his watch. His fist clenches in irritation. "Lady friend?"

"A poacher. I have the feeling he's stood me up again. I went to see Athman Mamar at the clinic. He told me about your visit, but he refused to comment on the fire in his workshop."

"That's the way it is in the upper echelons. You torpedo each other to death, all friendly enemies, but you don't share your little problems with the *hoi polloi*. Can I ask you an inappropriate question, captain?"

"We're colleagues, after all."

"How come Comms hasn't asked about Alla Tej's transfer?"

The captain raises an eyebrow. His smile flares what's left of his nostrils horribly.

He leans on my shoulder and confides, "It's a question of technique, *kho*."

I nod distractedly, telling myself I've heard that somewhere before.

Chapter eleven

The night hides behind its blackness. The city digs in behind its *portes-cochères*. Noises remain silent and the silence hears itself holding back. The weather doesn't allow you to breathe. Sonofabitch, we're at war! Time to learn some respect.

A powerful car glitters at the corner of the street. Vast as an empire, it's polished so well that it glows almost as far as the gleam of the street lights.

It stops in front of us. A door opens, and the mountain gives birth to a mouse. Despite his dinner jacket and his eight-inch cigar, the nabob could just as easily have walked under the chassis without stooping, but, highly conscious of his social standing, the man takes the trouble to walk around his Mercedes.

Ewegh and I are standing up against our truck, arms crossed in front of our chests. The dwarf considers us like a temple guard finding a turd on the sacrificial altar, pauses at the Tuareg's bulk, and shifts his lips to one side.

"Whose is this 'dozer, yours?"

"He's not a bulldozer."

"And this isn't a building site either."

I open my earns-too-little jacket to show my cop's badge.

"You are Abderrahman Kaak?"

"*Mister* Abderrahman Kaak, owner of the Raha hotels, CEO of Afak Import–Export, president of DZ Tourism. What do you want with me?"

His alcohol-laden breath corrodes my eyes, his gall my guts.

"We have some questions to ask you."

"About what?"

"We'd prefer to chat indoors."

"You're out of luck. I've mislaid my keys."

I say to Ewegh, "Sir has misplaced his keys."

Ewegh nods, climbs the steps, and staves in the door of the villa with a single kick. The dwarf quivers, shocked. He drops his cigar and his complexion turns gray. If we had kicked his own father up the ass, I'm sure it wouldn't have upset him as much.

"Hey! That door's a work of art! Really, where do you get off? That door cost me an arm and a leg."

I say to Ewegh, "It cost him an arm and a leg."

"We'll make do with the rest."

The little mite looks around him, mad with rage. His bowtie leaps about under his chin.

"You're mad!"

"Let's go in, Mister Kaak. We're better off with the ears in the walls than the ones in the satellites."

He looks us up and down and mutters, "As police officers, you're a disappointment. Your manners are no better than those of delinquents."

We bundle him into a living room twice the size of my one-bedroom apartment. He assigns us some sofas with a disdainful gesture, goes up on tiptoe to rest one buttock on the arm of an armchair, and places his doll-like hands on his thighs.

"Make it quick, I've got a bath to take."

Ewegh stays upright in the doorway, expressionless as a signpost.

I examine the paintings and weapons cluttering the gallery. Illicit fortunes all look alike, and like nothing else.

"Word is, you and Ben Ouda were very close."

"It's the truth."

"They don't understand why you weren't at his burial."

"I was in Paris being treated for a tumor."

"The word is, you were practically his main confidant, too."

"That's right."

"He surely must have talked to you about the threat on his life."

He raises his finger to his cheek in the manner of *The Thinker*, ruminates a moment, and stands up.

"Inspector…"

"Superintendent."

"All right, Superintendent, malicious tongues talk a lot but don't explain much, unfortunately. I suppose it's not where their talent lies. Ben Ouda wasn't quite himself recently. He had totally committed himself to putting a deal together. He had bet all his resources, including his mental ones. Bankruptcy took everything away. He became extremely depressed. He was convinced he'd been taken for a ride. He was a diplomat without equal, but businesswise he was hopeless. He refused to own up to the financial catastrophe. Instead, he tried to pin the blame on his associates. It was no longer comfortable for me to admit to knowing him."

"Makes sense. He was disappointed. His pals had let him go under."

"That's not right. Ben took the whole thing very badly. He saw enemies on all sides."

"Is that why he was trying to get revenge?"

"What?"

"Ben was thinking about writing a compromising book."

Abderrahman Kaak sits down opposite me, on a glass table this time. He seems relaxed.

"He just wanted to preach illusions, Superintendent. He went from this journalist to that writer and made them believe he was in possession of the document of the century. Rather than accept the clumsiness of his own investments, he heaped criticism on those who had succeeded where he had failed."

"And yet, someone panicked. We know, because someone did him in and ransacked his safe."

The gnome doesn't turn a hair. He looks at me with amusement, then puts his index finger to his thumb, making a circle, and blows through it. "He was bluffing…"

"Professor Abad believed him. He had even agreed to collaborate with him."

"I went along too, to begin with. I asked to see some proof. Ben made arrangements to clear out. I was forced to the conclusion that there was no proof. Ben never could hide anything from me."

I extract an index card on which I have copied, in capital letters, "H-I-V."

He reads it without trembling, purses his lips and says, "If you found those initials on your medical report, Superintendent, your troubles have only just begun."

"I found them somewhere else, on a step, next to Professor Abad's body."

"I don't know what it means."

"Not the slightest idea?"

"I'm sorry."

In the car, as we go down to Bab el-Oued, I ask Ewegh what he thinks of the nabob's performance. The Tuareg barely moves his lips.

"He delivered his lines well."

"That's what I think too."

※

"I'm going to have to perform my ablutions all over again," Lino complains as he rests his backside on the corner of my desk. "Kaak is a walking sewer."

Since his metaphor doesn't have the desired effect on me, he wipes his hands on his knees and adds, "I've gone through the archives with a fine-tooth comb. His file is dripping with filth. In '76 he's working as a ticket clerk in some movie house in the burbs. Disappears with the cash register. Sentenced to twelve months without remission. In '81 he opens a small business doing TV repairs in people's homes. Twelve months without remission for burglary. In '85 he's an authorized distributor for Sonacome. Arrested for dealing in spare parts. Case dropped. In '89 he's the manager of the Raha, a hotel on the coastal road. He's arrested on a morals charge. Case dropped. In '91 he sets up Afak Import-Export. He's arrested for importing tainted foodstuffs. Case dropped. By '93, his Raha company comprises five hotels, three five-star restaurants and three fast-food joints."

"Did he do all that with the proceeds from the movie-house job?"

"*Nyet.* His manna from heaven arrived in '83. He met up with one Dahman Faïd. He becomes his front man."

"Intellectual qualifications?"

"Wouldn't know a news flash from a commercial."

"That doesn't explain how he became a friend of Ben Ouda's."

"The dip used the Raha hotels. In those days, the bellboys didn't just carry your bags."

I push the buttock off my desk with a wooden ruler: the lieutenant is starting to block my light. Lino drops into the armchair and his face half disappears behind my telephone.

"He must know a thing or two, Super. Mustn't let go of him."

I lean my head against the back of the chair and put my feet back up on the desk. The cracks in the ceiling distract me. I close my eyes to think.

That afternoon, I go back to Abderrahman Kaak's place. Not only has he repaired the door, but he also hurries to protect it the moment our car parks in front of his grille.

"Did you forget something, Superintendent?"

"Maybe."

"I'm expecting guests."

"A female dwarf?"

"Much bigger."

"I don't see a stepladder."

He flushes to the whites of his eyes.

"Don't play games with me, Superintendent. I know my rights and the limits of yours. If you don't have a warrant, leave."

"Who needs a warrant when you've got a 'dozer?"

He puffs out his cheeks and steps back.

"What kind of benighted country is this, for crying out loud?" he complains, stepping in front of us again.

"The malicious tongues weren't convinced by your performance yesterday, Mister Kaak. I'm going to give you my version of events, and you're going to correct me if I'm wrong: Ben Ouda wasn't bluffing. I met him a few days before he died. He didn't give me the impression he was just rambling. He had actually had got his hands on something serious. A diskette. His problem was that he couldn't keep a secret. He went to see his great confidant, and that's when his troubles began."

At this, Abderrahman Kaak starts trembling and fidgeting. He clenches his jaws as well as his fists. He looks at Lino and Ewegh in turn, takes a step forward, and buries his finger in my navel.

"Get out of here, Superintendent. I've seen enough of you."

"Mister Kaak, if someone tells lies they must have a reason. I've checked. You didn't go to Paris, neither to have treatment for a tumor nor to buy some shoe inserts. You didn't go to your pal's burial because you thought he wasn't worth it. You're the one who betrayed him."

"You're rambling, Superintendent. Ben Ouda was my best friend."

"What do you know about friendship, Mister Kaak? A blissful alliance with lots of billing and cooing in a pink bedroom? A game of charades when you're not in a hurry? Ben Ouda stopped being your friend the moment he began sniffing around your dirty laundry. Maybe he didn't suspect that you were just as rotten as the others, that if you threaten the shark you risk the pilot fish's future too."

"I demand that you leave!"

A commanding voice interrupts us.

"What's going on? You can be heard from the street."

Dahman Faïd is in the vestibule, flanked by Carrottop and two other gorillas who are so ugly you'd think they had just fallen out of their trees. An icy silence falls on the room. I look daggers at my men, who have allowed themselves to be taken by surprise, before I turn to face the billionnaire.

"Well, if isn't Columbo. What are doing so far from your slum?"

"Taking in some air."

"So take a walk. This is a residential neighborhood. Domestic rows and brawling are forbidden. The people of this hamlet have divorced themselves from the smell and the promiscuity of the *souk*."

Abderrahman is relieved. He jostles me aside and runs to his redeemer. The billionnaire holds him off with a glance and, with a finger, tells him to stay calm.

"It's foolish to brutalize honest citizens, Superintendent. The police have better things to do. They're paid to rid us of fundamentalism. Instead of playing the fairground strongman, why don't you go and exterminate the *maquis?* Now, if you'll excuse us, Mr. Abderrahman and I have work to do."

I don't know why, but suddenly I'm at a loss for words.

Dahman turns his beads over and over in his fingers, his smile voracious and his eye glassy. Behind him, his henchmen are champing at the bit, ready for the order to devour us.

I say, "What do you think you're fending off with your beads, Mr. Faïd?"

"The urge to walk all over you."

"That's ancient history. Look out the window. The world is changing very fast. The law is rising again from its ashes. Another word out of place and I'll throw you in jail like a common crook."

Carrot-head tries a diversion. That's all Ewegh needs. His lyrical fist lets rip. When it comes to blows, I don't believe all the hawsers in the world would be able to hold him back. At first, Carrot-head thinks he's been involved in a highway collision, then realizes that's not it and collapses like an old curtain. The two gorillas' hands freeze a couple of inches from their guns, appalled by the cannon on display from the utterly amazing Lino.

Dahman Faïd snickers, not even slightly impressed.

I go up to him to take him on up close.

"You're just a benign tumor now, Mr. Faïd."

"Your lab tests are flawed."

"I don't think so. And there's something else. I can't stand fake believers."

"You've got a problem with my beads?"

"Exactly."

He starts making them dance around his fingers again. His grimace becomes more accentuated.

"I assure you I have faith."

I nod to my men to follow me.

Dahman Faïd's sarcasm pursues me:

"Hey, Columbo! Why won't you believe me? I have faith. True as my beads. Tell him, Abder, tell him I have faith." He lets loose a gargantuan laugh. "Columbo, it isn't God who made man in his image. Nature requires each of us to create his own god. I don't much care whether mine has a beard that's light-years old or terrible horns on his head. What counts is having faith in him... Hey, Columbo!"

I retrace my steps, aware of every movement, blessed by every drop of sweat on my forehead. I feel as though I've gone back thirty years, as though I'm reconnecting with that thing that used to spring from my chest in the form of slogans, that used to be so effective in preserving me later on, when, at break of day, I would set out to conquer the world. All of a sudden, the bogeymen fall apart, their omnipotence disappears; all that's left as they go by is the satisfaction you get from a lesson thoroughly learned.

Dahman Faïd realizes that I have grown in stature. He flinches. And just because of that moment of weakness, imperceptible though it may be, I tell him, "If you rant at fate, Dahman Faïd, that proves that whatever god you have created, you're as empty as bagpipes inside."

His Adam's apple is stuck at the level of his chin. I follow his eyes and ambush him at the moment he goes back to intimidating me. Our breathing mingles. You could hear the dust scratching against the tiles.

I turn round and leave, certain for once in my life, pulled the devil by the tail without getting hold of the wrong end.

Chapter twelve

The Belvedere is a fabulous place. Once upon a time, lovebirds from the elite schools used to come here in their convertibles to look at the sea and change their underwear. They were identifiable by the brightly colored scarves fluttering in the breeze and their cut-glass laughter. In the surrounding area, among the lamps and the twittering birds, there used to be dogs walking their owners, aging ladies on the arms of their gigolos, and on weekends, entire tribes swarming around the white tables of the dairy stands. Back then, the days were bright blond as summer. The girls smelled of jasmine and the urchins' eyes shone like a thousand jewels.

Today, the Belvedere hasn't lost much of its splendor. After a three-year eclipse, the lovebirds are back, except they do less changing. And the tribes that still dare to frequent the esplanade double-check where they put their feet.

Down below, the city's encampments are constantly being patched up. In the shimmering haze, it looks like a gigantic building site. Beyond the road to the airport the Mediterranean rests, taking its cue from the lapping of the waves. The boats on the water amuse themselves by pretending their anchors are fishhooks. It seems to help them wait.

But all this is happening behind my back. I haven't come to the Belvedere to bring back the good old days. This morning, an anonymous phone call reported a suspicious vehicle in the basement of Parking Garage B. It took us two hours to evacuate the area and get the cars out.

The vehicle in question is a taxi. It's parked under a pillar, and it has a flat tire. Lino and I are barricaded behind a concrete ramp at the other end of the garage. We're watching a bomb squad ferreting around in the jalopy, their flesh covered with grease, their movements surgically precise.

They manage to open a door, then the hood. No bomb. In the trunk, however, they do discover a stiff in a state of decomposition. Despite the stench and the marks of abuse on the body, he can be identified on the spot. It is Blidi Kamel, age thirty, married with four children. Formerly a junk dealer in El-Harach. He had been involved in the murders of Ben Ouda and Professor Abad.

The bush telegraph takes care of the rest. As soon as I get back to the office, I come upon Captain Berrah. He's gotten wind of our find before the boss has. He courteously removes his carcass from the comfort of the armchair and holds out his hand.

"News travels fast, I see."

"We've got a bald guy at Comms too. This is the third of Gaïd's men to be hit in thirteen days. At this rate, we'll soon have no work to do."

I invite him to sit down again and take the chair opposite him.

"That's because we're not allowed to get to work on our suspects with a blowtorch."

The captain offers me a cigarette and forgets to operate his lighter. He has aged noticeably. Lack of sleep has put bags under his eyes and is firing on the rest of his features at point-blank range. He picks up a satchel resting against his foot and shows me a photo: the face of a filthy schizophrenic, topped by a jailhouse scalp.

"There's your ordinary-looking guy, tall as a billboard. His name is Hakim Karach, alias Bosco."

This has an immediate boomerang effect. I hit my forehead with my palm. I am the king of the idiots. I grab the captain's arm and drag him behind me, straight to Serkadji prison, where Alla Tej is stuffing his face at the Republic's expense, regally oblivious of the rescheduling of our debt and the strictures of the International Monetary Fund.

Cell number 48 blights the end of the corridor, halfway between the caged ceiling light and the latrine. Alla Tej is sitting in the middle of the room like a fakir, hands on his knees, head in the clouds. At first glance, you would think he was in the middle of a yoga session.

"He's shutting us out," his guard explains, scratching his back with his night stick. "He says he's claustrophobic and demands some company. At the beginning he was in number 16. And everyone wanted to be in number 16. With him, there was no chance of getting bored. We were forced to isolate him so as not to make anyone jealous," he concludes with the sage air of a patriarch.

"We've come to keep him company. Thank you, you're dismissed."

The guard is a heroic pile of flaccidity topped by a placid mug. He has a moustache down to his chin, tattoos on his arms, and flies that reach up to his navel. His voice is soft, and when he speaks, his gut quivers like a jelly.

"I can stay if you like," he says affably. "You never know with savages like this. They respond only to force."

I smile at him. He understands that I won't be needing his services and goes away, tapping his nightstick against his leg.

I poke Alla Tej with my toe. He stirs lazily. When he recognizes me, his face undergoes a change.

The captain reclines on the mattress and crosses one leg over the other. His nails scratch the material of his satchel absently.

I take a step back and lean against the wall.

"Are they giving you a hard time in here?"

Alla shrugs.

"I wasn't any better off outside."

The captain begins to stir. He rolls up the photo of Hakim Karach in his fingers and sends it flying through the air with a flick. The photo flutters, turns over, and lands in front of Alla.

"We have nothing to say to each other. I've told you what I know and it didn't earn me any mitigation. In short, I'm not relying on the police anymore, just the courts. No point trying to intimidate me."

We don't say anything, the captain and I. Alla waits for a reaction, a sign that won't come. Our silence continues.

"You don't bother me."

He swallows under the opaque gaze of the captain and tries to provoke mine. In vain. In the corridor, the guard can be heard rattling his nightstick against the bars. A metal bucket overturns at the other end of the section and is immediately rewarded with a booming curse. Silence gains the upper hand again; heavy, unpleasant, it invades cell number 48. Alla hesitates; his hand timidly slides across the floor, circles around the photo, and pulls it over with a finger.

"Never seen the guy," he lies, to save face.

"It's Bosco."

"Don't know him."

"Don't make things difficult. We're all worn out. There's no point getting yourself thrashed like a donkey... Is this the same Bosco you told me about the first time I came and offered you a deal?"

Alla lifts the photo up to the light of the window, a symbolic gesture.

"What's in it for me?"

"I promise to assign him to your cell as soon as I get my hands on him."

"That's him."

"Did you owe him money?"

"That's right."

"Did Gaïd's group owe him money too?"

"He wouldn't even dare to think about it. Bosco's a nobody.

He can beat up hookers and kick down-and-outs in the ass, but he doesn't have the guts to stand up to Gaïd."

"He killed Ben Hamid and Brigitte two weeks ago."

Alla drops the photo contemptuously.

"That can't be him. You've got it wrong. Bosco's a small-time crook. He works in cabarets. He abuses whores and drunks, but he wouldn't know how to take on anyone else."

"He took out Zaddam and Kamel Blidi too."

Alla lets out a laugh as coarse as it is brief.

"You're barking up the wrong tree."

"And yet it's true."

Alla stops moving and places his hand on his chin. He looks incredulously back and forth between me and the captain.

"Now you're playing with me."

"No tricks."

He shakes his head several times.

"It's not possible. He's just a little piece of low-class shit."

"Gaïd used just to be a turd left behind on a patch of waste ground," says the captain irritably. "Now he's a big problem. We're not going to write an essay on the subject. What we want to know is simple: what's making Bosco chase after the Hairdresser?"

"Don't ask me—ask him. He works at the Majestic, a love hotel on the coast road."

"He's not there anymore. His employer hasn't heard from him for months."

The guard appears at the grille, stroking his nightstick.

"Did you call me, Superintendent?"

"Not really."

"I'm just over here."

"Noted."

The guard's moustache rises in a facial spasm and he then disappears.

Alla buries his head between his shoulders. His voice becomes a discomfited gurgle. "Do you have a cigarette?"

The captain sends over a pack of Marlboros. Alla frantically helps himself and starts smoking at top speed. We let him pollute himself for three minutes.

Finally, he says, "Gaïd killed the diplomat to get a document back—something like that, at least. He had been given an advance of a million dinars and was supposed to get another mil afterward, but as soon as Gaïd got hold of the thing he got big ideas. He wanted five times what had been agreed. The client wouldn't give in. A while later, Brigitte, who used to work at the Majestic from time to time, told Merouan TNT that Bosco had been recruited to get back the document. Nobody believed her. One evening at Riad El-Feth two guys held me up at gunpoint. They said Bosco wanted to see me. They picked me up bodily and threw me into a car. I managed to get away at a red light. That evening, you turned up at my place with your bone-crusher."

"Did you tell Gaïd your story?"

"I couldn't get hold of him."

"Who came to get you that evening?"

"Ben Hamid."

"Did you tell him about Bosco's men?"

"I told him the cops were passing themselves off as Bosco's men. That's what I thought when you turned up at my place."

"Who's the client?"

"Gaïd never talks about that with his men. He does his business in secret. That's his rule. He has a job, he carries it out. The less you know, the better."

"So he wasn't the emir," the captain cries.

Alla's mouth twists contemptuously:

"What's an emir, pal? All that stuff's just a distraction. It's like a whorehouse. You screw what takes your fancy, that's all there is to it."

Chapter thirteen

As if to shake off the decaying hovels on its verges, the road sprints on its belly toward a forest of eucalyptus trees. But steering clear isn't enough: the company you keep invariably catches up with you in the end. Lying in ambush around a corner, a *douar* catches it in the mesh of its shacks and reduces it to fragments. Yet the road manages to salvage a few streaks of bitumen and crawls another half a mile or so, tattered and much reduced, before giving up the ghost at one end of a small dock. Starting again at the far end, the surface skirts the hillside, crumbling dangerously, and blends into a rutted pier where the carcasses of cars rent out their guts to crabs and octopi.

It is midday. Apart from a ghostly fisherman atop a rock, the place would make an alley cat's fur stand on end. Among the parched grasses, the scuttling of a lizard is an event. There is a stench of heat and dead dogs.

At the end of a goat track, a tumble of shacks like wading birds allow themselves to be molested by the waves, facades peeling and windows boarded up tighter than the cage of a big cat.

Tahar Brik lurks in shack 28. You have to cross yourself to get there to appease the ancient walkway, which creaks if so much as a seagull sets foot on it.

Lino presses a rusty bell. There is no sound of ringing anywhere. He bangs on a windowpane. Curtain rings instantly click along a brass rail, revealing a woman's face, unfathomable as the ways of the Lord.

"We're looking for Tahar," Lino tells her.

The woman's expression remains inert, more like a figurative painting than a face.

After an eternity, she says, tonelessly, "Not here."

"We're friends of his."

This word doesn't attract her interest. She looks as though she's been hit on the head so many times she doesn't understand why suddenly nobody's hitting her anymore.

"We're from the police."

She raises the curtain slightly.

"Policemen, with hair like girls?…Get away from here. There's no Tahar here. My husband will be back soon."

"Look out," Ewegh warns us from the other end of the walkway. "He's escaping from the back."

We hear sounds of upheaval. Children start bawling inside the hovel. I run toward the terrace and arrive just as a parachute-shaped robe hurls itself into the void and plunges into the sea with a tremendous splash.

I rush down a gaping staircase and squelch through the murky effluvia of an open sewer. Meanwhile, Ewegh reaches the beach in huge strides, climbs a series of rocks, and welcomes the fugitive as the waves recede.

"No need to panic, my friend. We mean you no harm."

Tahar Brik puts his hands on his head. His *gandoura*, swollen with pockets of air, floats around him like a giant doughnut.

"We're from the police."

Tahar calms down a little. He stays in the water for a moment, pensive, then climbs up a rock, rejects the Tuareg's hand, and goes back up the staircase. In silence. He blasts me with an evil look, brushes Lino aside on his way, and goes back into his house.

We join him.

He has thrown a blanket over his shoulders and is sitting on a bench. His face is swollen with anger.

"If you've found me," he complains, "the others will find me too. Only the public prosecutor knows where I'm hiding."

"He's the one who slipped us your address."

He spits on the ground violently.

"They're all the same!"

Tahar is a small and swarthy fellow, communicative as a doornail. His frizzy hair is white at the temples. He must be about forty years old and have a whole heap of reasons for his eyes to burn like fire.

"All you had to do is summon me. Now the neighbors are going to ask questions. Do you give a damn about my safety, or what? I've shown remorse and I'm at the disposal of the law. There's no chance I'll run away."

"OK, we made a stupid mistake. Try to calm down."

"And then what?"

He wipes his nose incongruously with the blanket.

In the next room, the kids have stopped howling. Their silence is frustrating.

"We want to get our hands on Gaïd, and we're in a hurry."

"I've gone straight. I don't see how I can help you. I'm much more interested in saving my skin than feeding it. This is my thirteenth hideout in eight months of being on the run. I don't even go out to get a bit of fresh air. Gaïd's hot on my heels. He's killed my cousin, dynamited my house, and forced the rest of my family into exile. I didn't even go to the old woman's burial."

"Calm down, I beg you."

"You think that's possible? You turn up here with the heavy artillery, you stir up the whole village, and you want me to give you a round of applause. Where am I going to hide out now? I've got three epileptic kids and a wife who's gone to pieces, and nowhere to put them."

"We'll find you somewhere safe."

He thrusts his head back under the blanket and groans. His angular shoulders shake spasmodically.

"I can't take it anymore. I've had it. I'm going to kill the wife and kids, and then I'll slit my own throat."

He stretches out his neck and wipes the tears from his cheeks in despair. "Oh yes! That would be the best thing."

Tahar Brik goes on to draw up a list of hideouts that might be holding Gaïd the Hairdresser. I set up a surveillance system around each den and deploy a system of lookouts such that a SWAT team can be in place within twenty-odd minutes; then, ever the confident strategist, I wait a week for a light to flash on my onboard display.

On Friday, at 1900 hours, lookout number 8 tells me that a suspect vehicle has appeared near hideout "H" at Haï El-Moustaqbal. I give Lino the wheel and put Ewegh in the backseat and we charge in.

There are solemn baptisms. And then there are baptisms that are so stupid they don't even make your teeth grate. To baptize Haï El-Moustaqbal, "City of the Future"—an appalling collection of rotting hovels piled higgledy-piggledy on a wasteland overflowing with pestilential gullies and poverty—reeks of cynicism. Haï El-Moustaqbal doesn't even dare to hope. Its horizons are cursed. Its tomorrows are afraid. It's as if it sprang up out of a nervous breakdown. Not a streetlight, not a pothole; nothing but a stricken no-man's-land caught in a vicelike grip between the cowardice of one side and the neglect of the other. It is a zone given over to perdition of all kinds, where the people—neither subjects nor citizens—are born and die amid universal indifference.

Our lookout receives us on a terrace that's been turned into an observation post. He's an old man, on his way out, who has decided to risk death rather than endure life. He's one of the patriots who crisscross the areas contaminated with fundamentalism and keep us informed as to the pulse of the populace.

"The van's been there for an hour," he tells us, indicating the hideout with a bony finger.

I examine the courtyard through my binoculars.

"Who lives there?"

"The owner abandoned it last September. He has a son in the army. This is the first time anyone's shown up there."

"Might be the owner," Lino guesses.

"The vehicle was stolen by an armed man at four o'clock on the coastal road," the patriot says. "I intercepted the report on the radio."

Night gradually envelops the den of thieves. No light has been turned on in Hideout H. There are fewer and fewer noises, and the alleyways empty of people. A carter chastises his mule along the rutted way. His curses are lost in the call of the muezzin. We watch the area for two hours. Not a sign of life in the courtyard. We decide to go and see up close what's going on.

Ewegh disappears and goes to the far side of the hovels. Lino and I scale a cinder-block wall to avoid the courtyard. The house is as silent as a tomb.

I try the door handle. The click forces me to back off. We find a smashed window. Lino goes first. I follow him into a narrow, bare room. We follow the rough walls of a corridor and come out into another room. Suddenly, the ceiling light is switched on and an extra-large demon, livid and terrifying, is revealed. He's lying on a mildewed mattress, his torso naked, one hand to his bloody flank, a remote control in the other. His blood has soaked the top of his trousers, seeped into the mattress, and spilled onto the floor.

"Welcome aboard, Superintendent Llob," he says in a weakened but steady voice.

My hemorrhoids bloom abruptly, like a bunch of Barbary figs. I don't need to turn round to know that Lino is two contractions away from shitting his pants.

Gaïd the Hairdresser gives us a smile from beyond the grave.

"I've got a remote, and it's not for the TV."

"We get the message."

He groans; raises his head. His hand strokes his wounded side painfully.

I step forward.

"Sit!" he reacts. "There are three kilos of TNT underneath your carcass in the basement. I only have to press this thing and your own God himself wouldn't be able to put the puzzle back together."

I step back.

His shout has hurt him. He looks at me with hatred. The pain gets him going again. He clutches his wound but doesn't stop looking at us.

"How many liters of blood are there in the human body, Superintendent?"

"Depends how much there is on your hands."

He frowns. His jaws quiver all the way to his cheekbones.

"Unbelievable. I piss away my blood for more than six hours and I can't even pass out."

"Your time hasn't come. We'll get you to the nearest hospital."

"That's very kind of you, Superintendent, but I don't trust you."

His hand describes an arc. He curls up; the remote control drops out of his hand and falls onto the tiles. A film of ice freezes my spine. I can hear Lino trembling with panic. His heavy breathing puts a dent in the back of my neck. I finally understand what is meant by the phrase "caught like a rat in a trap."

"Look out, my friend, those toys are unpredictable."

Gaïd snickers. His fingers scrabble dangerously at the instrument of death and pick it up.

"I like your sense of humor, Superintendent. The great journey will be wonderful in your company."

"Put your device down and let's talk. The ambulance is all yours. You'll be taken care of just like any other injured person."

"I've already booked my place in paradise."

"Don't be a fool," says Lino in a strangled voice, panicking. "Think of the poor folk minding their own business nearby. You could blow up the whole neighborhood."

"Given the bitch of a life they have, I'll be doing them a holy favor."

His thumb strokes the remote control horribly.

Hallucinating, my throat dry and my chest constricted, I beg him: "Wait, wait. Don't do it, it won't do any good..."

"All aboard!"

This is followed by a massive detonation. I have the vague sensation of being stretched out at vertiginous speed. I am a comet created out of nothingness... I pull myself together. The first thing to reconcile me to the world of the living is the Hairdresser's shattered head. It is resting on the pillow, staring at me with a single glassy eye, a hole in its temple and another in its neck. Ewegh smashes the window with a shoulder barge, swings one leg through the gap and lands in the room, his gun aimed at the mattress. The detonation was him. Lino, meanwhile, hurries to empty the batteries out of the remote control. He is pale to the roots of his hair, and he is shaking like an old witch in a trance.

We go over the place with a fine-tooth comb and find neither a bomb nor a diskette. Gaïd was bluffing. He just wanted to die, and we helped him.

Chapter fourteen

W ell done!" roars the boss, beside himself. "Gaïd was finally in our hands and you let him get away. Just like that, stupidly. He took us all for a ride. Now we're back to flying blind. Nice work. You can be proud of yourselves."

He strides up and down his office, turns out some ashtrays, harasses his swivel chair, tugs violently at the curtains. I watch him put on his act and pray that he'll smash his fist against the wall or slice his hand on a tile. I've been killing myself for half an hour, explaining that my men and I weren't supposed to know whether Gaïd was bluffing or not, but the boss refuses to listen.

"Shut up! There's nothing more to be said. Thanks to your carelessness, Police Central is isolated from the rest of the world. Comms won't do us any favors. The chief of staff hung up on me…" He brandishes his newspaper in my face. "It's on the front page of all the papers. Nobody believes our version. As far as the whole country is concerned, the police murdered a key witness in cold blood. *Who wants to bury Ben Ouda twice over?*" He shows me the headline that takes up more than half a page. "We don't have the right to make mistakes. Even if you'd been blown up alongside him, the doubt would still have lived on after you. We're suspected of complicity, Mister Brahim Llob, of stacking the deck. The only way to get us in the clear was to arrest that son of a bitch and keep him alive to stand trial. He was *meant* to be heard. That was the plan. Ben wasn't just anyone. He couldn't just be killed by some joker for any old reason. Remember the escalation, the day after his murder. We didn't look to complicate things. The system is there for a reason, we decided. And we are the system. We stand accused of fucking things up, of doing a dirty job. As always."

He changes tack and charges over to me. His mouthwashed breath assails me and his carefully manicured finger digs its fingernail into my belly.

"I warned you, Llob. This case is nitroglycerine. It needed to be handled with kid gloves."

"It's not the end of the world," I say, exasperated. "The inquiry isn't over. With Gaïd or without him, I'll carry it through to the end."

"And how, pray tell? The Hairdresser was our last trump. Everything hung on that goddammed diskette and we don't know where it is."

"That's my problem. It's my turn to cause the maximum ruckus to flush out our prey. I demand carte blanche."

"I don't have anymore of those, needless to say. You'll have to use your own credit card. And bogus expenses won't be reimbursed."

❧

Abderrahman Kaak appears in my office like a genie summoned by the magic word. He's in a foul mood, almost ridiculously so. Flushed, a whitish froth at the corners of his mouth, he raises himself up on the points of his shoes and slams some papers down on my desk.

"I have a passport, a visa, and a plane ticket. I'm not the subject of judicial proceedings of any kind. I'm not under house arrest. I'm perfectly in order and therefore absolutely free to move as I wish. So can you explain to me why your little friends at the airport refused to let me take the plane to Lyons?"

He has spent the journey from the airport to the central police station rehearsing this tirade. I know because he recites it in one go, without taking a breath.

I spread my arms fatalistically. This gets him fired up all over. His tiny crimson jowls quiver. He raises himself up another notch and threatens me with his monster baby finger.

"You haven't heard the last of this, I warn you. You're going beyond your authority, Superintendent. I have friends in high places. I promise you, your goose is cooked."

His nostrils flare with anger.

He comes back down on his heels and disappears.

"It's intolerable," he protests, offstage. "Shit, this is a republic! The law's the law, after all!"

"There are several you can use, Mister Kaak."

I lean forward over my blotter to focus his attention and count on my fingers. "There's the law you cut to measure, there's the law you use as a doormat, there's the law you wipe your ass with…"

The nabob can read in my expression the unconquerable aversion I feel toward his particular kind of garbage. This takes the wind out of his sails somewhat. His hand smoothes down the front of his jacket. It's his way of calming things down.

He tries a different tone: "I have an extremely important business appointment in Paris."

"And how is that my problem?"

I tap my fingers on a bulky report and confide, "You're in the shit up to your neck."

He shrinks another four inches.

"There's enough in this file to chase you all the way to hell. All my life I've been waiting for the chance to trump some rotten apple of a nabob. Today, I can do it. I'm going to take you apart bit by bit, *Mister* Kaak."

Ordinary mortals can sometimes get cold feet; Abderrahman Kaak has ice all over his. The blood has left his face. His eyes are glued to the floor. His hand fumbles uncertainly in his pockets; he brings out a handkerchief and wipes the back of his neck, under his chin, and his forehead.

He doesn't say anything. He asks to see, first.

I show him a business card.

"We found this among the things of Gaïd the Hairdresser."

"My hairdresser's name is Tony."

"I'm talking about the terrorist."

"Never heard of him. Anyway, I'm not in contact with fundamentalists."

"What the hell was it doing among Gaïd's belongings?"

He comes over to the desk, takes the card from me and runs his fingers over it. That's enough for him to recover his composure. The tension fades away from his features. He returns the card to me and moves away again, relieved. "This card is from the Hotel Raha-les-Palmiers."

"You're the owner."

"Not anymore. I sold it more than eight months ago. Along with the Raha-Golf, the Raha-les-Pins and the Raha-les-Sablettes… Besides, this card doesn't prove anything. You'll find them in tourist information offices, hotels, anywhere. Hotels are public places. Business cards are advertisements. People give them to you. I hope you haven't made me miss my appointments in Paris for something as pathetic as this."

"Mostly, there's this, Mister Kaak," I say, tapping the report again.

"I'm sure it's just a misunderstanding."

I wave a sheet of paper under his nose. "I have the right to keep you in for forty-eight hours."

"In that case, I'd like to speak to my lawyer."

"He thinks you're in Lyons."

"This isn't proper."

"I don't give a damn."

He gestures in an attempt to appease me.

"I'm sure we can deal out the cards again, Superintendent."

"I misdealt on purpose. I kept the good cards for myself and removed a few of yours."

He protests and starts waving his arms about and fulminating. Ewegh wraps him up with two fingers and leads him to the debating chamber, a six-square-foot closet with a low ceiling and depressing walls, furnished with a metal chair, a spotlight, and a table.

Abderrahman Kaak sits there for twenty minutes, waiting for someone to come and grill him. Half an hour later, he rests his cheek in one hand and starts drumming with the other, his eyes glued to the reinforced door.

The boss joins me in the room next door, from which we can observe the suspect through a one-way mirror. He tells me the phone hasn't stopped ringing in his office. Kaak's friends are worried. I suggest he tells them their protégé has probably been kidnapped by terrorists and that with a bit of luck we'll find his body in a stairwell tomorrow. The boss finds my cynicism unhealthy and reminds me that what I've done is against regulations. I reply that I've had to adapt to current practices. He smiles and promises me his umbrella if a few tiles come loose in the storm. I reassure him by telling him that a tile on the head would probably straighten my ideas out.

Around midnight, the nabob rebels. Having taken off his tie and jacket and rolled up his shirtsleeves, he runs at the door and starts ruining his shoes against it.

At two o'clock in the morning, he cracks, collapses over the table and falls asleep.

I persecute him: "On your feet, in there! Police custody isn't a bowl of strawberries."

It's all Kaak can do to stop himself breaking down in tears. He's at the end of his tether, his features are blurred, his hair disheveled. His eyes, half rolled up into his head, meets mine with the tenderness of a jellyfish. He wipes his face with his hand, tousles his mane, and examines me at length.

"I'm going to take this matter to the very top," he breathes.

"I'd be glad to rent you my own private elevator. In the meantime, spit it out. If you think you haven't stewed long enough yet, I can come back later. I'm in no hurry."

He stops me with an outstretched hand. "Let's get it over with. I want to go home."

I sit on the corner of the table and rest my clenched fists on my knees.

"Ben was my friend," he begins after long reflection. "He was different. The others, they were either suckers or they were out to make a profit... I got on with Ben. That didn't happen to me very often. Despite my success, I was still just a poor boy from the slums: poor background, poor in mind and body... True, I didn't do badly for myself, but Ben added a certain ethical dimension to my good fortune. It gave me a kick, being friends with a well-known man of letters—me, the former ticket clerk in a low-rent movie house... With Ben, money was just money. There was more to life than that. Ben was a different kettle of fish. He had class. He had talent.... Naturally, I felt sorry for him sometimes, but it had nothing to do with pity. In a town that thinks only of its digestion, geniuses are sadly out of place. I understood him. I respected him. I would never, ever, have betrayed him. He was my one saving grace."

He examines his fingernails sadly. His chin digs into the void like someone unearthing intolerable memories.

"He was bored to death. He came back to this country full of ideas. His life as a diplomat had fed him illusions. He didn't understand why we rewarded predators in this country rather than visionaries. Ben was an idealist. He liked to say that there was no worse apocalypse than a culture in crisis. He spent his time organizing book signings, exhibitions, intellectual get-togethers—but it was always the same story. People weren't interested in his efforts; they made fun of his good offices. The few curious people who gathered around him only turned up to see if there were any angles to be worked, and then they didn't come anymore. It wore him down, and so as not to come off as crazy, he began to take a leaf out of their book. He threw himself into business. And there, too, he was unlucky. He discovered a different apocalypse: fraud. For a guy who dreamed of a land of milk and honey, it was the last thing he needed. I think his tendency toward vice grew out of his disappointment. He was punishing himself. He must have felt unworthy of his vocation.... After October 1988, he thought the coming of democracy would give him a second chance. He was at all the meetings, at the heart of the discussions. Debate inspired a good many of his initiatives. He started writing like a man possessed. *Dream and Utopia* was a trigger for him. Success was fatal. He felt exhilarated. He had sworn to make a fresh start and to go even further…. And one evening, he rolled up at my house at some impossible hour, over-excited, unrecognizable. 'I've got it!' And he waved a computer diskette at me. It was his philosopher's stone, the document of the century, the accursed copy of the Fourth Hypothesis…."

"The Fourth Hypothesis?"

"I bet you haven't deciphered the initials on your index card yet, from the other evening…HIV… In roman numerals IV means four, hence H4 is the Fourth Hypothesis…. Ben explained to me that it was all about a devilish plan hatched by a group of well-heeled opportunists to help themselves to the industrial base of the country."

"Meaning?"

"That's all he told me…. I wasn't particularly interested. I can't stand complications. Ben was skating on thin ice. Already he was none too popular. The politicians had put him in quarantine. The businessmen were trying to ruin him. The intellectuals despised him. Ben was alone. They had it in for me because I received him at my home."

"Who had it in for you?"

"Everyone. My most loyal supporters avoided my hotels as a mark of protest. My backers closed their lines of credit. Ben had a talent for getting people on his back. I begged him to go to Europe. He wouldn't listen."

I clasp my fingers together, lean forward a little, and ask him, "You didn't tell anyone about this document?"

"It would have been very careless of me."

"Who do you think could have betrayed him?"

"He could have done it himself, without realizing it. Writers are so naïve."

I touch my moustache with a finger and think for a moment.

Kaak goes back to examining his fingernails, as worried as before.

"While he was giving you the lowdown on the Fourth Hypothesis, he didn't mention any names or refer to any individuals?"

Kaak raises his head and leans gently back in his chair. He purses his lips. First he shakes his head no.

"I have no right to quote anyone, Superintendent. Ben showed me a diskette, an ordinary three-and-a-half-inch diskette. It could have been blank. I can't afford to compromise people just because Ben couldn't stand them. You're a cop: if the document really exists, you find it and do with it what you will."

"Dahman Faïd was mentioned."

"Don't push it, Superintendent. I may be a right bastard, but I know my limits. When I'm not sure of anything, I never take a risk."

"Okay," I say, raising my hands, "I won't persist. Ben Ouda talked to me about a codename: N.S.O."

He stops me immediately, partly to show me that he's understood and partly to show that he's willing to cooperate.

"That's the New Social Order, as foreseen in the Fourth Hypothesis. A series of draconian measures, announced by the rich men in question, to impose their new economic order. Since the transition from a façade of socialism to a free market can't be made without a few breakages, the interested parties put themselves in charge of the breakages. According to Ben, every last bug had been ironed out. The plan provided for every eventuality and foresaw a range of actions to be taken to meet all contingencies head on. Sabotage, blackmail, corruption, and assassination all featured in due form in the HIV directive, because that's what it was: a real directive."

"Do Athman Mamar's misfortunes have anything to do with—"

"Stop! No names, please, Superintendent. Besides, I think tiredness is beginning to play dirty tricks on me. I'd like to go home, right away."

Chapter fifteen

Athman Mamar is in his swimming pool, which has been converted into a physiotherapy suite. I recently visited a clinic for the war wounded; it wasn't any better equipped. Chrome appliances sparkle in the half-darkness, pretty enough to make you want to injure yourself so you can make use of them: fitness machines, some with weights, others with cushioned seats; sophisticated prosthetic devices connected to control panels; any amount of high-tech equipment; a whole panoply of gadgets, arranged like an assembly line, enough to heal a legless cripple.

Our patient, up to his neck in the water, is advancing along a ramp. His knees give way from time to time and he stumbles. His nurse, a massive black man dripping with sweat, crouches over him, arms ready.

"That's very good, sir," he says encouragingly. "Another twenty feet and we'll take a break. Don't look down. Keep your eyes on the diving board. Don't just rely on your arms. Your legs need to work too."

Mamar nods obediently and carries on cheating. He can't help it. From where I'm standing, I can see him working his arms and dragging his legs.

He stops under the diving board to catch his breath and pick up a bottle of mineral water. As he puts the neck of the bottle to his lips, the torture victim catches sight of me. An electric shock would not have shaken him more violently.

He puts the bottle down without taking a drink, somewhat annoyed by my bare-faced cheek.

"Who let you in?"

"The draught."

The giant pushes against his knees and stands up. His massive, thick-veined muscles bulge. He rests his clublike fists on his hips, tenses the slabs of muscle in his chest, and fixes me with a stare, ears pinned back slightly, awaiting the order to reduce me to sausage meat.

"Leave us, Babay," says Mamar soothingly.

The giant grinds his teeth in protest. He gathers up his T-shirt, throws it over his shoulder, and disappears toward the changing rooms.

Mamar glides over to the steps on his left and reclines on them. His acrobatics have tired him out, and it takes him two minutes to catch his breath. His body is covered with the ghastly-looking reddish stains of his burns.

"Have you been there a long time?"

"About a quarter of an hour. You're doing well. I didn't think you were going to make it at first."

"The odds have improved…and I thought I told you to stay out of my hair. You're jeopardizing my convalescence."

"You told me that? I forgot."

I grab a wheelchair, turn it around and sit in it.

"Look at this," I observe. "Truly revolutionary. Dashboard, gear stick, horn, rearview mirrors. The only thing your hotrod doesn't have is a stereo system. Where's it imported from?"

"It's local and it's available. Do you want one for your old age?"

"Don't think I can afford it."

Mamar dries himself carefully with a large cotton towel, avoiding the scorched areas of his body.

I steer the chair around the swimming pool, slalom through the medical arsenal, perform a few creative stunts, and then park beside the diving board.

"Amazing!"

"What do you want, a medal?"

"I had a look at the report on the fire in your workshop. Your business looked like it was going belly up. You were about to file for bankruptcy. The report suggests you probably blew the place up to pocket the insurance money."

"You forget that I went up with it."

"Not everyone's good with explosives."

Mamar gives himself a horrible wound on his shoulder as he wraps the towel around his neck.

"Don't take advantage of the rough patch I'm going through, Llob. My doctors have advised me not to get upset. I need all my strength to climb back, do you understand?...True, my workshop had been in a slump lately. I was short of raw materials and my suppliers wouldn't bail me out. But from that to blowing the place up, that's worlds apart. I had three billion's worth of machines. You don't wipe out a fortune for the sake of certain poverty."

"Your machines were practically useless. They were junk."

"That's what you say. I had started renovating my park less than a year ago."

"Renovation? That's not mentioned in the report."

"Let's say I haven't had the time to straighten things out with customs."

"I see. A black-market shipment."

"I've had a look at the report too," he says hurriedly, to change the subject. "To show you I have nothing to hide, I managed to get hold of a copy."

"That's illegal."

"Perhaps, but it's perfectly feasible. As for the investigation, it's worthless. It reeks of a cover-up. It's not serious. Irrelevant. Not even enough to interest a corrupt judge. If you must know, someone wanted to kill two birds with one stone: eliminate Athman Mamar and ruin his family."

"Do you have any idea who that might be?"

"An idea's not worth much. But I'm keeping it for a rainy day."

"Why do people wish you harm?"

"Rivalry, my dear Llob. Living space, bloodsucking, investment, leadership…"

"…Fourth Hypothesis…."

Bingo!

The uppercut hits Athman when he's least expecting it. He throws his head back, stunned. But he recovers fast. His life as a hardened, unrepentant swindler has made him take shocks very well. He doesn't even bother to shake his head to clear it. He puts out a hand to request time out, then his fingers curl again, leaving only the index finger pointing at me.

"This conversation is over, Superintendent."

He claps his hands.

The giant returns at a gallop, nostrils steaming. I go quietly, but in a hurry.

⁂

As I leave the swimming pool, I emerge into a huge garden. I run for shelter in the shade of some foliage: the sun is white hot. I haven't even reached the path across the courtyard when a voice calls out to me as if from a dream. "Mister Llob?"

I turn around.

A half-naked siren is watching me from a balcony. She is exiguously dressed in a filmy robe, her hair is black and straight, and her long pink leg would make a monk think twice before returning to the monastery. Her adorably puffy eyes show that she has just gotten out of bed.

She is Madame Mamar, and she is more beautiful than the scurrilous stories circulating around the city would suggest.

"Leaving so soon?"

She stands at the top of her tower, weight on one hip, checks whether the coast is clear, then indicates a spiral staircase.

"Would you like to come up for a minute?"

"With my rheumatism, it'll take far more than that to climb those stairs."

She giggles. A breath of air tugs at the edge of her robe. Madame Mamar has left her underwear behind on the bedside table. She continues to dance on the spot while I reach her altitude. Her clear-skinned hand seizes mine and draws me to her. Her perfume goes to my head, and I have a lot of trouble keeping it attached to my shoulders. She leads me into a lavishly decorated bedroom and pushes me onto a couch.

"I heard what you were saying, you and my husband."

She kneels in front of a tray and pours me a cup of coffee. As she turns, her robe opens and her firm, tanned breasts almost tumble out onto her arms.

"My husband isn't well. Testing the wheelchair wore him out. He used to be a very active man."

"I've known him for ages."

"Well, the man you saw tottering about downstairs is not the man you used to know. He's in pain, and he thinks he's had it. I hope it's not asking too much if I beg you not to get him agitated. He's already tried to do himself in once."

"I'm sorry. I didn't know."

She stands up and spreads out on the edge of the bed. A beauty spot the size of a pea adorns her right thigh. I can't take my eyes off her.

Her expression softens.

"We all live our own kind of hell, Mister Llob. Luxury doesn't protect us against the rough edges of the outside world. We suffer the tragedy just like everyone else. It's cruel to witness the martyrdom of your country."

"I don't doubt it, ma'am. It must be tough to hold a barbecue on scorched earth."

She winces.

Her hand retrieves part of her robe that has slipped a long way, and puts it back over her knee.

"You don't seem to like rich people, Mister Llob."

"Not all of them… Thanks for the coffee."

She grips my wrist to stop me getting up.

"I'll try to keep it short, Mister Llob. My husband is a businessman. In the world of business, there's only one Mecca: the stock market. And only one article of faith: get a return on your investment, always get a return on your investment. Sometimes you abandon your principles. You have to grease palms, tread people underfoot. But there are limits to everything. And my husband knows when to stop. He's a patriot. He's always put the country's interests ahead of his own."

My snicker doesn't escape her.

She hates me already.

"What I mean, Mister Llob, is this: We didn't set fire to our workshop to pocket the insurance money. Somebody tried to out-and-out murder my husband, just as they executed my own brother, Professor Abad—because we refuse to go along with people who wish our country ill. I don't know exactly what it's all about. My husband doesn't confide in me. But I'm a woman, and I notice things."

Lot of help that is!

I put down my cup and stand up. She doesn't try to hold me back. Our eyes lock together, searchingly. I wipe my mouth with a napkin and, for no good reason, aware of my tactlessness and unable to justify it, say, "You should cover yourself, ma'am. There's nothing worse than a summer cold."

Her expression changes abruptly. I feel her hatred in the bottom of my soul. She doesn't get up to come down with me. She stays on the bed, tense as a cobra. Her behavior gives me goose pimples. Even if she is not a justification for the hostility I feel toward people of her class, she is a good example of why I don't give them my trust or my sympathy. The cool of the greenery is unable to reduce the torrid heat of the glare planted in my back. I envisage Madame Mamar on her balcony, a gash in place of her mouth and her eye sockets filled with molten lava. I reach the gate and pause. I'm racked with the desire to turn around; I don't give in.

I get back to the sidewalk and my car. I start it up. The gears grind pathetically. I move off immediately, forcing a pedestrian to swerve out of my way so as not to be run over.

At the bottom of the street, I turn right, go down an avenue of stylish villas, cut down a neighboring street, and end up in a boulevard. The heat has forced people to go to ground in the cafés. Apart from a few cops standing rooted to the spot, the terraces and sidewalks are deserted.

As I stop at a red light, a Mercedes invades my rearview mirror. Its smoked-glass windscreen masks the driver. The light turns green. The Mercedes stays on my tail and doesn't go away. I don't begin to worry until I'm on the highway. After the Kouba exit, unease settles on my mind definitively. I rip the gun from under my belt buckle and place it on the passenger seat, just in case.

I accelerate, overtake a long line of beaten-up cars, and insert myself in front of a truck. The big car puts on a sprint to catch up to me, goes past me a little and slows down. The guy in the back-seat gives me a strange sort of a wink. Suddenly, he's brandishing a machine pistol. I press the brakes. My tires screech at the same time as the storm breaks. Fragments of glass shower around me like a cloud of flies. I lie flat. Behind me, the truck roars before running straight into the back of me. Just as I remember the steering wheel, the road surface disappears and I'm surprised to find myself about to hit a billboard. I turn a hard right, drift sideways, hit a barrier, regain control, and proceed across country for a while before wrecking the differential against a milestone. The truck miraculously misses me and plunges into the ditch. Through a cloud of dust, I can see the Mercedes straightening up on the hard shoulder. Its rear lights come on. It comes back toward me. My gun has disappeared. I look for it under the seats, cursing, and find it behind the pedals. I pick it up by the butt and try to get away. My door is jammed shut. I clamber across the passenger seat and fall out the other side.

On the highway, the scene is like a bullfight. The sound of furious horns is drowned out by the crunch of collisions.

The Mercedes stops about a hundred feet away. The guy with the machine pistol settles comfortably into a crouching position and sends over a lengthy burst. My car dances about under the shower and settles onto its punctured tires. The guy continues to spray my so-called protection, coolly, casually. He empties the magazine, loads up another. A flicker of flame appears under the hood and spreads quickly; a fitful fire starts under the engine. I go down on one knee and fire three times. One bullet hits the guy in the shoulder and makes him drop his weapon. This time, I stand up and take proper aim. His skull splits like an overripe pomegranate. He collapses, facedown in the dust.

Another joker comes to the rescue. He fires, forcing me behind the gathering flames. I return fire without causing him any bother. He picks up his companion and drags him over to the Mercedes, covering his retreat with short bursts. The big car skids off the gravel and bounces onto the Tarmac with a deafening roar.

The fire, meanwhile, is consuming the seats of my jalopy. Wild tentacles leap out of the doors and roll around the body, converging on the fuel tank. I run for cover behind a mound. The shock wave of the explosion hurls me into a shrub.

In the distance, the sirens of the SWAT teams howl. There is chaos on the road. I can hear men shouting and women screaming. Some ten vehicles have been involved in the pileup. There are people running in all directions. Eventually, I notice the blood on my shirt. A piece of glass has cut my wrist. It's the least of my worries. I'm satisfied: I've managed to flush out my prey.

Chapter sixteen

Herding animals have an unfortunate tendency: if one of their number suddenly gets a hair up its ass, the whole herd panics too, to the point of following it over a cliff.

The next day, Captain Berrah contacts me by telephone to say he's waiting for me at 9, Cité du Beau-Plaisir, a little bit of paradise a few hundred feet from Sidi Fredj. The address transports us to a private area hidden away behind a copse of trees. The villa in question is set in a clearing: delightfully pretty, with finely chiseled blue stones and a mane of ivy. A gilded gate stands open before a tiled courtyard spiked with bunches of greenery trimmed like punk hairdos. I park the car beside a fountain made of Italian marble guarded by an ancient cannon, evidently pinched from a Spanish fort.

The captain greets me from the veranda. He tilts his chin at a Mercedes half in and half out of the garage.

"Is that the one?"

"Same license plate."

"There's blood inside."

He notices the bandage on my wrist.

"Nothing serious, I hope?"

"It's just for show."

He laughs with a nasal sound and precedes me into the interior of the building. We go up a staircase carpeted in red. Comms officers are turning the place over in silence.

Bosco is slumped on a sofa, his shoulders hunched and his chin on his chest. Something has taken a crater out of the back of his neck. A shattered vertebra can be glimpsed through the burst flesh, and a pool of blood, black and coagulated, glues his shirt to his back. A glass lies at his feet; in drying, the contents have left a yellowish stain on the carpet.

"They rubbed him out while he was enjoying a pastis," says the captain.

There are powder stains all over the back of the sofa. They shot him from behind at point-blank range. Bosco wasn't expecting it. The expression on his face immortalizes his surprise, which must have been as great as it was brief.

"He had this in his pocket," the captain adds, holding out a key. "No papers, no coins."

It's a cast aluminium, Fichet-Bauche lock, the key attached to a three-inch metal plate with a number engraved on one side and a logo on the other.

"Does the logo mean anything to you?"

"It belongs to a firm that specializes in installing lockers. They handle the luggage storage areas of stations and airports exclusively. They gave me a list of their customers."

"No diskette, of course."

"I'd have been surprised."

"Me too."

We start with the main railway station, then the bus stations. Three hours later we find what we're looking for at the airport, in basement level c. The key turns smooth as silk in the lock of a wall-mounted locker, and the door opens to reveal a brand-new leather satchel.

"Make sure it's not booby-trapped first," the captain orders a specialist officer.

After the usual safety precautions, we take the satchel out.

Among the clutter of cassettes, envelopes, and bits of paper, the first thing that hits me in the pit of my stomach is a carefully bound manuscript on whose cover someone has written, in large red letters, HIV.

The captain and his experts get to work as soon as they get back to headquarters. They will spend the night wearing out their eyes and gray matter over the documents. At about eleven in the morning, I arrive at their operations room, which has been set up in a small lecture hall. I find Captain Berrah exhausted and disheveled, with bags under his eyes and blue lips. His exhausted men are scattered among the thirty-odd chairs raked up to the level of a projection booth.

"I hope you haven't wasted all this energy on a wild-goose chase, Captain?"

"It's been a hundred percent worth it. Sit down over there. There's some coffee and sandwiches."

He claps his hands to thank his men. "You've been great, guys. Back here again in two hours. There'll be a lamb roast in the mess tonight."

Once we're alone, he collapses into an armchair and fans himself with a file folder.

"Good stuff?"

"Better believe it!"

"And Dahman Faïd? I'll be unhappy for the rest of my life if he's not in the frame."

"Up to his neck, Superintendent. Up to his neck."

Only now do I allow myself to pour myself a cup of coffee and bite hungrily into a sandwich.

Berrah paints a succinct picture of the Fourth Hypothesis and has me listen to some tapes. I listen and listen and can't believe what I'm hearing. Dahman Faïd, the billionaire Kaddour Abbas, Jilali Younes, owner of the Le Mouflon department store, the jeweller Hamma Dib and two other wealthy men have been putting the finishing touches to the chapters of the HIV directive and putting a rope around their own necks at the same time. Here and there it begins to sound like an auction, as some of them claim this or that sector of the economy while others make concessions so they can rush in to demand something else in return. They speak of tactics to be adopted, the wisdom of certain commitments, the need to unleash a wide-ranging program of sabotage. Berrah illustrates the presentation with a list itemizing infrastructure targets. He shows me photographs of Merouan TNT dynamiting the steel foundry at Zitouna and Hamma Dib's henchmen carrying out their dirty work. We watch irrefutably compromising videotapes, examine photocopies, sort the exhibits. There's enough here not only to write a bestseller but also to put six of the wealthiest men in Algeria in front of a firing squad. It's all there: from details of a conspiracy to destabilize the national economy so badly that the state would be forced to sell off some of its industrial wealth to the comprehensive list of sectors coveted by Dahman Faïd and his cronies; from telephone conversations to copies of checks for astronomical sums made out to pyromaniacs and murderers; from the death sentence passed on Ben Ouda and other "black sheep" to written reports on successful missions.

"When do we arrest these bastards?" I ask, disgusted.

"After I've had my beauty sleep."

"I know this is Comms' collar, but I'd like to take care of Faïd personally."

"No problem, as long as you bring him straight here."

"You're a gentleman. By the way, do you have anything on Athman Mamar?"

"And how! He was in on it from the beginning. Apparently his brother-in-law, the professor, gave him the lowdown on Ben Ouda's plan. He pulled out. Faïd got Merouan TNT to blow him up along with his workshop."

I hold my chin between my thumb and index finger and think. The captain glances at me, struck by my frown of concentration.

"Something wrong, Superintendent?"

"I don't understand. Did you have a mole in there?"

"No."

"So who put this whole show together, and why?"

The captain is disconcerted. He frowns and stops fidgeting.

In my opinion, it hasn't for one second occurred to him to ask the question. Proves that sometimes he lacks proper technique too.

Chapter seventeen

The secretary is daubing powder on her nose as the elevator releases us into the hall. She hastily adjusts her décolletage and greets us.

"Gentlemen?" she chirps with a professional smile.

We pay her PR no attention and go past her with a clatter of boots. She hits the roof, almost leaping over her desk and running over to stand in our way.

"Mister Faïd is in a meeting. It's strictly forbidden to disturb him."

Alerted by her squealing, Carrottop shows his ground-meat face at the end of the corridor. When he sees us, his hand instinctively goes to his revolver.

"Uh-uh," says Ewegh warningly.

Carrottop gulps and takes his hand away. The secretary struggles to hold us back. We drag her along in our wake, totally deaf to her entreaties.

"You can't go in," yaps Carrottop.

"Buzz off, you sphinx," Lino cautions him, revived by Ewegh's presence.

We jostle past the Egyptian, the bimbo and the gigantic oak door, invading the meeting room. A bunch of suckers, ripe for the plucking, is gathered round a huge mahogany table; they turn as one toward the commotion. At the far end, Dahman Faïd pushes his glasses back with a finger, appalled.

"We're sorry," sobs the bimbo. "We tried to stop them."

Dahman Faïd doesn't say anything, but his blazing eyes pass over us like flamethrowers: mean, destructive, ruthless.

"The meeting is adjourned," I say to the suckers, who don't seem to understand what's going on.

They turn to their head honcho, more and more disoriented. Dahman Faïd makes an imperceptible movement of his head. The suckers obey. They gather up their napkins and papers and make their escape in a rustle of disappointment. The secretary leaves backward, pale and on the point of tears.

"You too, Egyptian," Lino barks.

Carrottop shifts from one foot to the other to show his boss he's with him for better or worse. Ewegh seizes him by the scruff of the neck, sends him flying into the hall, and slams the heavy door shut.

"You can be sure, Mister Faïd, that we haven't gone to all this trouble just to get the diskette back. We're not interested in it anymore."

"Where do you think you are?" he says, just as I'm beginning to think he's swallowed his tongue. "In a cattle market? Did you wipe your crummy shoes on the mat? Who gave you permission to come in?"

"The law, Mister Faïd."

He tears off his glasses and throws them down on his blotter.

"What law? Do you know who you're talking to?"

"To Dahman Faïd, a fat, filthy piece of shit who pollutes the atmosphere enough for two Chernobyls. I'm here to put your ass behind bars."

He grabs the telephone and punches the buttons with a furious finger.

"Put the phone down, sir. That won't work anymore. The days of get-out-of-jail-free cards are over."

"Who fed you this horseshit, Columbo?"

"My stable boy."

"Demagoguery, nothing more. You shouldn't take all these consciousness-raising campaigns so seriously. That's for the rabble, Columbo. It's all for show. You don't make a revolution with flashy slogans that don't mean anything."

He grabs his beads and wraps them around his wrist.

"Go ahead, Mister Faïd. Call your friends."

"For something so trivial? You must be joking. My guards will take care of throwing you out."

"It's over, Mister Faïd. Your own dog would cut you dead. You've gone too far. It's the end of the line now: all change."

He leans back in his throne and clasps his fingers over his ogre's chest. A contemptuous smile hovers on his lips.

"You're the one who needs to come down from the clouds, Columbo. Your show's only on in Europe now."

"It's true, we're in Algeria. And Algeria, Mister Faïd, is like gold: the more you rub her, the more she shines. She's a home fit for Olympians. She lowers her guard sometimes but never her knickers. And the more you back her up against the wall, the better she fights."

"That's what they taught you in the boy scouts."

He disgusts me.

"I'm arresting you, Mister Faïd. Only God knows what a strange effect that has on me. I arrest you for the murders of Ben Ouda and Professor Abad. I arrest you for the attempted murder of a superintendent of police in the exercise of his duty. I arrest you for breach of national security. In short, I'm arresting you so that life can go on without having you underfoot."

His own feet land on the desk explosively. He throws his head back and lets loose a huge laugh that shakes him from his chest to his throat; the laugh of an all-powerful hydra that refuses to believe misfortune has befallen it. Suddenly, he interrupts his bellowing and his face contorts itself into a horrifying mask. His lips pull back, forming a cannibalistic leer. He holds his arm out toward the bay window on his right.

"There isn't a single corner out there that doesn't know who

Dahman Faïd is. Half the city belongs to me. Most people live there thanks to me." He claps his hand to his chest. "Me! I'm the one who made this city what she is today."

"A bullring."

"A real capital, modern and ambitious. I built her, stone by stone, flagstone by flagstone. I gave her the best years of my life, put my entire genius at her disposal. It's my cash that flows through her veins, it's my sweat that waters her gardens, it's my investments that make her heart beat faster than a virgin's on her wedding night.

"Look at her. Look at her well, and you will see that she has eyes for no one but me, for no other god. Between us there is a passion that laughs at all taboos. We have no inhibitions, none at all. We are one. This city is mine. I've always refused to let her fade. And God knows how many stupid slogans have tried to sully her name, how many low-class pretenders have tried to seduce her, how many donkey trainers have tried to sell her off cheap. But I said no. Thanks to me, she's more beautiful than ever. My Algiers the White isn't an odalisque; she's a sultana in her own right. She needs pomp and ceremony. She needs lovers and courtesans. She needs people to make sacrifices for her, to dare, to curse, to create and to destroy for her. That's the only way to serve her, the only way to deserve her. She is a work of art. You make sketch after sketch, but afterward, it is she who makes masters of us, who raises our talent to the level of the holy.

"Alas! this kind of poetry is wasted on you, Columbo. What is this, an orgasmic privilege for a pathetic, barely alive cop like you? What's it like so high up, for someone who gets vertigo whenever he stands up? What do you know about *building*, what do you know about posterity? Nothing. Goodness me, you know nothing. *Glory only resonates in a soul that is worthy of it.* Mayakovsky got it wrong: the night is wild and feverish and a race of giants made me what I am so that I would have a purpose. Do you understand? So that I would have a purpose. Unlike you. Squeaky-clean shadows lurking in the wings. Pathetic, a gut with legs, puffed up, full of yourselves."

"You should find yourself a new optician, Mister Faïd."

I nod to Ewegh to suggest that the man needs a straitjacket. The Tuareg holds out the handcuffs. Dahman Faïd is stunned. The sight of the cuffs is traumatic. He stares at them incredulously, looks at his purple wrists and refuses to imagine them constrained by these grotesque rings of metal, rusty and demeaning. With the force of an earthquake, he finally realizes what is happening to him. He shakes his head in denial, several times, convinced that a bigshot of his stature is exempt from this kind of ritual, that he will escape from life's upsets, that he is indestructible, immune.

"Don't come near me. I forbid you to place those microbes on me. I am Dahman Faïd. I have the authorities eating out of my hand. Famous people prostrate themselves at my feet. I order you to leave, I dismiss you, I excuse you…"

I've seen a few poor devils lose it. I've seen people hallucinate all the way down into despair. I've seen some gods fall on their faces. But the show put on for us by Dahman Faïd goes way beyond anything else. I have just witnessed a panel from the Apocalypse.

Chaper eighteen

The flunky receives me obsequiously, relieves me of my cigarette, and leads me into a colonial-style drawing room. He's an ancient old geezer, thin and upright as a maypole, with a face like a knife blade and a fleshy hooked nose at its center resembling a flag at half-mast. The stiffness of his upper body and the tail of his frock coat make him look like a washed-out flamingo who's stepped in a snake's mouth and is trying to pretend there's nothing wrong. I suppose his excessive dignity helps him perform his domestic chores philosophically.

"If sir would be so kind as to wait for me here," he intones, like a broken record. "I will inform sir that sir is here."

He comes back in a minute, still as inflexible as an obsession. His shoulder drops reverentially and his white-gloved hand shows me the way.

"If sir wouldn't mind following me."

"Lead away!"

We traverse a universe carpeted in dark red velvet and sparkling with silver objects. Stuffed animals watch me from among overstuffed sofas and small tables cast in bronze. A genuine coat of armor stands guard in an alcove, helmet closed and sword sharpened. There is even a Bengal tiger, mouth open in a roar, which seems to be offering its flattened hide to the soles of our shoes, fresh from a session with a steamroller.

Abderrahman Kaak is lounging in a rocking chair on the veranda. He looks like a marionette left behind by a famous ventriloquist. He's holding a cigar in one hand and a glass of alcohol in the other; he's contemplating the sea, soothed by the creaking of the chair. He doesn't turn around. His cigar directs me to another rocking chair. I occupy it, careful not to end up with my legs in the air; I place my foot on the balustrade and let my arms hang down beside the armrests.

"Lovely day, don't you think, Superintendent?"

"For those who have the means."

"This is my favorite place. When my morale is low, I sit here and the Mediterranean takes care of the rest. An aperitif?"

"I'm a believer."

"A soft drink, then?"

"I'm trying to get rid of a sore throat."

He nods and puts his glass down on a small glass table. I have to sit up to see him, because he's totally hidden in the bottom of his chair. He's wearing an embroidered desert robe, with gold sequins on the collar and silk curlicues on the sleeves. His tiny chest is shiny with perspiration, like the shell of a turtle. A solid gold chain reflects the sunlight onto his fleshy neck.

He taps the ash off his cigar.

A few paces away, the sea rolls exalted waves in roaring foam.

"Two hours ago it was dead calm," he says.

"The wind has changed."

"Is that why you're here?"

"Can't hide anything from you."

I install myself comfortably in my seat and give it a little push to make it start rocking. The rocker starts up with a relaxing creak.

"I must admit that you have a lot of imagination, Mister Kaak. You've orchestrated the situation like a maestro. Will you offer me a cigar?"

"Do you think you deserve it?"

"I do."

"Well then, help yourself."

I take a cigar from a carved box, clip off the tip, and light it with a platinum lighter.

The first puff makes my brain tingle. The second almost makes me drunk.

I look back at the leaping sea and start narrating:

"Once upon a time there was a man, rich as Croesus, whose rapacity was matched only by his compulsive greed. He was a gifted businessman and practically lived for scams. The only problem was that he lived in a place where lucrative opportunities were far too rationed, stifled at birth even, by a trash-heap socialism that was well-versed in the arts of corruption. Our tycoon had to perform acrobatics, often degrading ones, to follow his vocation. It wasn't enough to buy friends in the *nomenklatura* that could never shelter him from changes in the texts of the moment or ideological harassment. In those days, if a private development dared to disturb the lethargy of the proletariat, the whole country immediately cried heresy. It was better to be poor; all wealth was suspect, even devilish. And Dahman Faïd discovered the trick: instead of building big and providing a focus for protest, why not invest a little bit everywhere, enlarging both your living space and your room to move?…He shrewdly opted for a system of front men."

Beside me, silence.

I pull on my cigar to bring it back to life and continue:

"Abderrahman Kaak didn't turn up his nose when he was approached. He was a notorious ex-convict, an unhappy, suicidal boy from the slums. He leaped on the chance eagerly and then discovered the life of the chateau, the cruises and privileges of the nabobs. Not every day, though. He often had to take the fall for his boss. A front man lends his back, too. That's in the fine print of the contract. The big bosses don't get their hands dirty. They prefer to leave the dirty work to others. No matter: things were going great guns for Kaak until the day the country was hit by the fundamentalist epidemic. War moved in on Numidia. A tragedy, of course, but for a certain well-heeled minority it was a godsend. A perfect opportunity to stop the mouth of this dime-store socialism that was preventing initiatives from developing into fortunes. To do that, it was necessary to support the hotbeds of tension, to throw fat on the fire and disorient the country so that it could more easily be duped. It became imperative to trap Power into suing for mercy, to give up its proletarian principles, to make significant concessions."

"Crazy! Rich people are incorrigible!" says Kaak ironically.

"Wait to hear what comes next. It's not over. Now that privatization, Power's main concession, is official policy, Dahman Faïd doesn't need front men anymore. He starts reclaiming his hidden wealth so as to build big. That's how Abderrahman Kaak's misfortunes began, as he saw his empire of facades crumble at Faïd's whim.

"Forced to sell seventy-five percent of the Raha hotel chain and thirty-five percent of TZ Tours so that Dahman can buy up the steel foundry at Zitouna, Abderrahman goes mad. At this rate, it won't be long before he's back on the skids. 'What the hell,' he says to himself. 'So I'm a front man, so what? On paper, officially, administratively, legally, I'm the owner! All I have to do is get rid of DF and it's all over.' And that's where you showed your remarkable intelligence, Mister Kaak: you got rid of Dahman Faïd within the rules of the game. Without getting your hands dirty. Without compromising yourself... Since DF is mixed up body and soul in the wave of bombings, why not denounce him? You're in the same firm. You know everything that goes on. You started snooping right away, recording, filming and photocopying until the day came when you had enough evidence to put DF in front of a firing squad. So you write a courtroom drama which you develop around Ben Ouda, a fallen diplomat, an intellectual to the point of folly; someone who craves the limelight so badly he's prepared to crucify himself on the footlights if it will get him out of the wings. He would have done anything for a bestseller, Ben. He was the perfect dupe."

I notice that my cigar has gone out.

Beside me, Abderrahman has stopped breathing. For a moment I think he's left. I raise myself a notch to see. Kaak hasn't left. He's there, his glass in his hand, staring at the sea like a child at the aquarium.

I say to him, "You went to Ben to mesmerize him with your documents. Then you arranged things so that you could present him as threat number one. Dahman Faïd took the bait. The plan started, and this was the appalling spiral."

Abderrahman Kaak puts his glass down and leans forward to sit on the edge of the chair.

He turns, finally.

He has aged!

He looks at me strangely. I feel as though he is searching me high and low for a response to my story; he comes back empty-handed and takes refuge in examining his hands.

"You shouldn't have run off with the cash register from the movie theater, Mister Kaak. That was a very bad idea."

He nods.

I confide in him. "From the beginning, I asked myself who would benefit from the elimination of Dahman Faïd. A mole looking for promotion? An insatiable rival? An heir who needed to pay for the good life? No one was better positioned than his main front man. It was the evidence itself. It leapt out at me."

His fists clench and disappear behind the flap of his robe. His breathing catches, becomes more marked, sounding like the hissing of a cracked boiler.

"When we held you in custody, that was so that a special Comms team could stuff this house with microphones. I was inspired by your methods. All your calls are recorded here,"—I wave an audio cassette under his nose—"including the conversation with Bosco, the appointment you made to meet him at 9, Cité du Beau-Plaisir. You went there to assign him a mission. Then you killed him with a bullet in the head and stuck a locker key in his pocket, attention: police."

The trembling begins in the soles of his feet, climbs to his calves, pours into his thighs, and reaches his shoulders. Abderrahman Kaak is just an icy fever now, a quivering heap of uncontrollable wheezing.

"You thought you'd blow us away with those documents. It might have worked. But it didn't work. The ugliness of the rat doesn't make the toad any less repulsive, *Mister* Kaak, and dressing like a valet doesn't hide the monkey's grin."

He is standing, uncertain, pale from head to foot. He clings to the balustrade so as not to collapse.

He inhales very deeply to get his breath back and says in a tremulous voice, "My mother used to tell me that if you kill yourself remembering every little thing, the thing you forget is something big."

"Your mother was a poet, Mister Kaak."

"I'll get changed, and then I'm all yours."

"Go ahead."

His eyes are no longer of this world. He reels as he turns, unsteady among the pillars of his fortune, and knocks over a stuffed gazelle, unable to find his way in his own house. He goes into his room as if in limbo, his arm outstretched, his eyes rolled up in his head.

By the time the shot rang out, I was already walking toward the beach.

Glossary

douar—small county village

fellahin—peasants

gandoura—tunic

haj—loosely "Sir", term of respect for someone who has made the pilgramage to Mecca

harissa—spicy sauce

hammam—hot, public baths

kho—"Brother"

maquis—underground fighters

mujahid—one who takes active part in a Jihad

nabob—rich and powerful man

souk—open market place

taghout—tyrant; title for those in power, the military and police

About the Author

Yasmina Khadra

Yasmina Khadra is the pseudonym of Mohammed Moulessehoul, an Algerian army officer born in 1956, who adopted a woman's pseudonym to avoid military censorship. Moulessehoul held a high rank in the Algerian army, and despite the publication of several successful novels in Algeria, only revealed his true identity in 2001, after going into exile and seclusion in France. He is uniquely placed to comment on vital issues of the Middle East, Algeria, and fundamentalism. Newsweek acclaims him as "one of the rare witnesses capable of giving a meaning to the violence in Algeria today."

Khadra's previous books, *In the Name of God*, *Wolf Dreams* and *Morituri*, have also been published in English by *The* Toby Press.

The fonts used in this book are from the Garamond family

Other works by Yasmina Khadra
published by *The* Toby Press

In the Name of God

Wolf Dreams

Morituri

The Toby Press publishes fine writing, available at leading
bookstores everywhere. For more information,
please visit www.tobypress.com